I0617588

ORACLE
DREAMS
TRILOGY
BOOK 2

Shadow DREAMS

TERI BARNETT

Shadow Dreams
Oracle Dreams Trilogy: Book 2
Published Internationally by Teri Barnett
USA
Copyright © 2019 Teri Barnett
teribarnett.com
Lucky Crow Press

Previously published as Shadow Dreams
by LBF Books (an imprint of Lachesis Publishing Inc.)
© 2010 Teri Barnett
Significantly revised and re-released as Shadow Dreams by Lucky Crow Press © 2019

Editor: Joanna D'Angelo
Exclusive cover design © 2023 Joanna D'Angelo
Interior design © 2023 Indie Book Designer

All rights reserved. The use of any part of this publication reproduced, transmitted in any form or by any means, electronic, mechanical, photocopying, recording, or otherwise, without the prior written consent of the author, Teri Barnett, is an infringement of the copyright law.

PRINT ISBN 978-1-7328138-5-4
EBOOK ISBN 978-1-7328138-4-7

This is a work of fiction. Names, characters, places, and incidents are either the product of the author's imagination or are used fictitiously, and any resemblance to any person or persons, living or dead, events or locales is entirely coincidental.

For my dad and mom, Frank and Margaret Barnett
You are both deeply missed

CONTENTS

PROLOGUE

Near Paran
The Plane of Keilah

"We have a visitor, Ma'am."

The High Priestess Liazar licked her lips in anticipation as the guest was ushered into her chambers. She moved quickly to her simple, carved wooden chair, and sat down. "My, my. What have we here? Come, stand in front of me child. I'd like to have a better look at you." With long, thin fingers, she motioned to the girl, her pearl and garnet ring glistening in the candlelight. "How old are you, Cherub?"

"Seven, Ma'am."

Liazar openly displayed her pleasure with a wide smile, her teeth shining in the candlelight. Seven! So young! Surely, the little one had many years ahead of her. She looked the girl over, admiring the sweet rosy cheeks and long silver-blonde hair.

"What do they call you?"

"Sarah, Ma'am," the child answered solemnly. "Sarah M'Doro."

"And you have no kin here in Paran?"

The girl wrinkled up her forehead as she thought. "Well, there is my mother. And my grandfather. Papa died long ago. I don't remember much about him."

Liazar looked sharply at her maid, Esther. "I told you to bring only orphans, didn't I?"

Esther glanced down, studying the squat shadow she cast onto the floor. "I'm sorry, Ma'am. When I found her playing in the woods, I assumed she belonged to no one. Who would let their child run free like that?" She rushed over to the girl as quickly as her bulk would allow and knelt at her side. "But she is a pretty one, isn't she? Just look at the life in her eyes."

The High Priestess shifted in her chair. This was a dilemma. If there were relatives to miss the child when she didn't return home, there could be trouble. She looked again at Sarah, feeling her need growing. Of course, the absence of one child could be easily explained, particularly if she were left to run alone. Perhaps wild animals might have dragged her away. Liazar smiled again. She leaned forward, her long red hair spilling over her shoulders.

"Come nearer to me, Sarah M'Doro."

Sarah hesitated for a moment. Esther gave her a little shove from behind. "Go on, girl. You don't want to make the High Priestess angry now, do you?"

Sarah shook her head. Slowly, she took a step toward Liazar. She stopped, the candlelight casting deep shadows around her slight form. "I'm afraid. Please let me go home."

"Now, now, Cherub. There's no need to fear. I only want to give you a hug before I send you on your way." Liazar reached for the child. "Is that all right with you?"

The girl shrugged her shoulders. "I suppose that would be all right. As long as you promise."

"I promise I will let you go as soon as I've hugged you."

Sarah moved to stand directly in front of Liazar. She held her arms out, innocent, waiting for the embrace.

Liazar sucked in her breath as she noticed the downy softness of the child's skin and the long lashes that brushed her cheeks. She raised her hands and placed them on either side of Sarah's head, the thumbs resting over the girl's eyebrows. Murmuring quietly, she closed her eyes and uttered an ancient incantation.

Suddenly, Sarah swayed and fell with a soft thud to the thickly carpeted floor. Liazar opened her eyes and took a deep breath. "Put her form with the others, Esther," she bade. "Take care she's kept safe."

As the maid carried the child away, Liazar eased back into the chair, smiling. She lifted her hands, feeling the flushed warmth of her face and the firm, smooth skin. Blood pounded in her temples and her heart raced. The transference was complete. She now possessed the little one's soul and the years it had left to live.

Soon, she thought, *soon I will be immortal!*

PART ONE

CHAPTER ONE

The rain poured down, beating incessantly against the freshly turned dirt. Small rivulets formed, carrying the water into the excavated pits of the Diggers, the ones who searched for historical artifacts for their world.

"We should stop for the day," one of them grumbled.

"I'm soaked clear through to the bone," another joined in. "Ian," the man called to the expedition's leader, "can we hit the tents?" The workman gestured with his head toward the small encampment.

"Hold up a minute. I found something," he called back as he unearthed a metal object. "Bethany, come take a look at this."

Bethany M'Doro stepped carefully over the grid of strings that marked the area where the Diggers were working. The ground was slick, and she had to be careful not to slip and fall into one of the holes. Reaching Ian Johns, she ducked under the tarpaulin covering his work area and squatted down at his side, feeling a comfortable familiarity in his presence.

Ian, tall and solid, had been at her side as long as she could remember, through the birth of her child and the death of her husband. Now they worked side by side. She felt a great kinship for the man she called friend. He handed her the medium-sized silver filigree box he had just discovered. She gingerly turned it over in her hands, carefully washing the red mud away with water from a nearby bucket.

"Did you find the key?" she asked, noticing the container was locked.

Ian shook his head. "What can you tell me about it? If there's anything worth saving inside, I don't want to destroy the contents trying to get it opened."

She closed her eyes as several of the workers gathered nearby, eager to hear what the woman had to say about their latest find. Knowers always accompanied them on the digs; they used their ability to read the vibrations left behind on an artifact to tell of its previous owner. This was one of the more important parts of an excavation as it was the Digger's duty to help the people of Paran learn of their past through the science and magic of archeology.

When Bethany opened her eyes again, the light topaz color had turned a deep azure blue, a sure sign to the men and women around her that she was in the Knowing. She ran her fingers over the elaborate carvings of the box.

"This contains a manuscript," she started. Then the expression on her face turned from wonder to fear as hundreds of cuneiform letters ran through her mind. "I thought this was only a legend," she whispered.

"What is it, Bethany? Tell me what you see," Ian demanded.

"It's the Book, Ian. The Book of Eitel." According to legend, the Eitellans were a fringe group who practiced in secret, stealing children and young adults away from their homes, never to be seen again. Some said they lived forever and still roamed the forests of Paran.

"That's impossible. The Eitellans are the stuff of myth. A story told to make children behave."

"I know this well—my own mother would threaten to sell me to them when I misbehaved." She smiled, her eyes misting at the memory of Mama and how she always tried to be strict. She shook off the melancholy. "But I tell you, real or not, this is what the Knowing says about this box. Were there any other items with this?"

Ian motioned to one of the workers. "Hand me that bucket over there."

When the worker returned, Ian spread a cloth on the ground. Then, he slowly poured the contents out in front of Bethany. He looked through the dirt and stones until he found a woman's hair comb. He handed it to the Knower. "Only this. It was located in the layer above the box."

"Was there anything else?"

Ian leaned over and began sifting the soil between his fingers.

"Well, if you look closely at the composition of this dirt, it looks quite a bit like there's ashes mixed in. I sifted through some of it and I think there are bone particles here as well, but I can't be certain."

Bethany nodded. She scooped up a handful of the dirt and closed her eyes, waiting for whatever images presented themselves. But there was only darkness. "It's no good, Ian." She brushed one hand against the other, cleaning the dirt away. "There's not enough substance left to the bones for me to be able to identify them." Bethany turned her attention to the comb, moving her fingers over the thin tortoise shell teeth and the slightly raised mother of pearl inlay. This time, the images came.

"I want you to have this, Elizabeth." A tall man, with thick black hair and piercing eyes, handed the comb to a woman. "I love you," he whispered.

"Thank you. I'll wear it always," Elizabeth replied, a smile playing about her lips. She rolled her long brown hair into a knot on top of her head and fastened it with the comb. Turning her back to the man, she bade, "Unfasten the buttons for me, Connor. I'd like to show you just how thankful I am."

Connor ran his hands along Elizabeth's arms in a sweeping caress. He paused at her back and began to remove her dress.

Bethany shook her head to clear it. "I feel like I'm eavesdropping," she whispered.

"I couldn't hear you, Beth. What did you see? I've never seen you looking this… this… embarrassed? Is that the word I'm searching for?" Ian asked, his lips twitching.

She glanced at him, irritated at his amusement of her discomfort. "Don't be ridiculous," Bethany answered, a little too quickly. If Ian expected her to admit to something, he'd have a long time waiting. She held up the comb. "I'll tell you what I saw. This belonged to a woman. She had long brown hair. Also tall and thin. It was a gift from a man." She took a deep breath and looked around at the circle of Diggers. "She's not native to our land. Her clothing is strange."

Bethany paused as she struggled to interpret the new images that began spinning before her mind's eye.

A light flashed bright in her vision and Bethany unconsciously held up her arm, shielding her eyes. There, within a Paranian kiyolo, a sacred cave deep in the earth, the same woman who had received the comb appeared from nowhere. It was as if she came on the very wind itself.

Elizabeth looked around. She was in an altar room. In the middle of the space sat a large stone statue. "An odd place," she commented, looking over the figure. "I never saw anything like it on Earth."

Then, as if she only just remembered her purpose in coming, she clutched the box to her breast and spoke words that were foreign to Bethany. When Elizabeth was finished, she held the container out in front of her and admired it. "There now." She smiled. "If anyone opens you, they'll die for certain. A curse you'll carry until I say otherwise."

Suddenly, another light flashed, and a man appeared at her side—but it wasn't the same handsome, intriguing man Bethany had seen Elizabeth with earlier. He was much plainer, much paler, and didn't look at all well.

"Oh, Michael," Elizabeth cooed, "I'm so happy you decided to join me." She wrapped her arms around his neck and pulled him to her. Kissing him soundly, she continued to murmur endearments softly into his ear.

Michael pulled away slightly. "I don't know about all of this, Lizzy." He looked around the room. "Maybe we shouldn't have come."

"No, no. Don't say that. Think of all the riches we'll have. And immortality, Michael. We'll live forever." She glanced over to where she'd laid the box down. "I've memorized the book. It tells how."

"I've got a bad feeling. Open up that book and say the words that'll return us to Nevada. Please."

Elizabeth rested her head against his chest. "I'm not going back, Michael," she said, her voice low.

As Elizabeth spoke, a light flashed, and the room filled with flames. Michael screamed. The vision ended with the sounds of Elizabeth's laughter.

Bethany sat still, her face ashen. Never had she heard such a bloodcurdling scream. And that laugh; as long as she lived, she'd never forget it.

"Are you all right, Beth?" Ian asked. "What else did you see?"

Bethany ran the impressions through her mind again, focusing on the details. The kiyolo looked like the ancient meeting caves the group had just finished digging earlier in this moon's cycle. Most of those caves appeared the same on the surface. It was the secrets they held within that made each one different. The kiyolo's location wasn't far from their current site and would explain why the book was found here.

The woman's manner of clothing was indeed strange, foreign actually; a long, ankle length dress with high neck and long sleeves. Her hair, piled high on her head, was held in place by the comb. She'd mentioned something about Earth. Bethany shook her head slightly. No one could travel from there to Paran. Moving between the planes was simply not possible. According to legend, a person would incinerate. Of course, that could explain the final flames that engulfed the pair.

"I need some more time to study what I saw. What I *can* tell you is that she said something about the Earth plane. When she came here, she brought the manuscript with her." She leveled her gaze. "And she didn't come alone. A man followed. It looked to me like they both died after their arrival. The entire kiyolo went up in flames."

"That'd explain the layer of carbon we scraped off the ceiling during our excavation. But the Earth plane? C'mon." Ian caught Bethany's eye. He cleared his throat. "Oh, you're serious. Can you tell us anything else about her?"

"Only that her name was Elizabeth. She placed a curse on the box. Whoever breaks the lock will die." Bethany closed her eyes. When she opened them again, they had returned to their normal topaz color.

LATER THAT EVENING, Bethany and Ian huddled near the fire under a handspun woolen cloth. It was getting late in the year and the time for winter was drawing near. The rain had stopped and Bethany ran her fingers through her long blonde hair, trying to dry it out.

She and Ian had grown up together. He was her best friend and her rock, always there to support her and her work. Since the death of her husband Joseph, five years ago, Ian had become even more protective, almost to the point of stifling.

He loves me, and I love him, but not in the same way. He is more brother than anything else.

She looked up at him, the stubble of whiskers on his firm chin glinting red in the firelight. She shivered and he put his arm around her, drawing her close. His presence was comforting. *What am I going to do with this man?* Bethany asked herself, half smiling. *I don't want to risk our friendship by becoming lovers.* Besides, she just wasn't ready to give her heart again.

And then there was Sarah, her daughter, who was currently tucked away safely with Bethany's father while Bethany worked. The child had suffered deeply after Joseph's death. They both had. She was grateful for Papa and his healing ways.

Bethany closed her eyes and again saw the men dragging her husband's body from the cave they were excavating. If only there had been a small flicker of life left, she could have saved him. The healer in her was strong, but even she could not surpass death.

"Are you all right, Beth?" Ian asked.

When she didn't answer, he hugged her tighter and stroked her cheek. He tilted her face to his; and she heard his breath catch at the sight of her face. It was a full moon, and she literally glowed with the light it cast, her hair radiating like a halo around her head. "You're on fire," he whispered huskily.

Bethany looked at him. Realizing what he was saying, she wrapped her hair into a tight knot, fastening it in place with the tortoise comb they had found earlier. One of the signs of a Knower was that they drew the moon's light from its source with every fiber of their being. The night's glow, combined with the fire, permeated her translucent skin. "I wasn't thinking," she murmured.

"Don't be. It's part of your heritage. You're beautiful." He lowered his mouth to hers.

For a brief moment, she considered what it would be like to kiss him. Before their lips could meet, she pulled away. "I can't do this, Ian." She looked up at him and their eyes met. "I love you, but not in the way you want me to."

"I'll take your love any way you'll give it," he replied, moving closer again.

She turned away, focusing her gaze on the fire. "Ian, I—"

Ian pulled back. "Sorry, Beth." He ran a hand through his shoulder length auburn hair and shook his head. "I was lost in the moment."

Changing the subject, he continued. "So, what do you suppose all of this means—the Book of Eitel, the man and woman from the Earth plane, the particles of bone and ash?"

"I don't know. It seems like all of our legends are coming alive with this find. My guess would be the bones belong to this Elizabeth and Michael. The myths say no one can survive traveling between the planes, and I saw a fire rise up around them at the end of my vision." Bethany shook her head. It was inconceivable, even to her—someone steeped in legend and lore—to imagine that people could actually travel between the various planes of existence. If true, a world of possibilities were opening before her very eyes as she imagined what might be found. No. Best to keep both feet on the ground. It was the only way to solve this mystery. "Maybe I'm wrong about the box and its contents. What do you think?"

Ian met her eyes. "In all the years I've worked with you, Bethany M'Doro, your Knowing has never been wrong. We need to get that box open, if we can find a way to do it without anyone dying. The manuscript will answer our questions."

"I don't think we should tamper with it until we've put more information together." Bethany picked up her heavy clay cup from where it rested near the fire and took a sip of hot bitters. She inhaled deeply of the orange and cinnamon scent. "We should find one of the old Weavers. There has to be one who can spin the stories of Eitel for us."

Ian nodded. "They could hold a clue."

"That's what I was thinking. Especially the ones about the Eitellan's ways of worship." She looked up at Ian. He was studying her closely. "There's something I didn't mention to you before when I was reading the box. In my vision, Elizabeth arrived in a kiyolo. It looked quite a bit like the one we excavated earlier this cycle."

"Why didn't you tell me?"

"I'm telling you now." Bethany shrugged. "I didn't want to alarm the workers. Considering how superstitious they are about the Eitellans, I was afraid of scaring them more than I already had."

"I guess I'll forgive you that one, Beth." He smiled. "You know, I'm beginning to wish I had paid closer attention to my grandmother when I was a child. She knew all of the stories of the time when this sect ruled Paran." Ian rubbed his hands near the fire, warming them. "Do you know any Weavers?"

"No, but I would imagine my father does. When we head back tomorrow for supplies and to check on Sarah, I'll talk with him."

CHAPTER TWO

The next morning saw the sun shining brightly, chasing away the stormy haze of the previous night. The large conifers dripped sap mixed with rain, their clean aroma filling the air around the excavation site. It was the sound of this gentle rhythm, hitting the roof of her tent, that roused Bethany. The last snatches of her dreams worked through to the forefront of memory and she saw the woman, Elizabeth, again.

Bent over a cooking fire in a small wooden structure, Elizabeth stirred a pot of soup. The door pushed open and a man walked in, closing it gently behind him. It was the same man, Connor, who had given her the tortoise comb.

"Evening, wife," he called as he hung his hat on a peg near the door. In two strides, he was at her side. He leaned over and placed a light kiss on her cheek. She didn't turn toward the man, but only kept her attention on the meal she was preparing.

While she cooked, Elizabeth kept glancing at a small timepiece on the fireplace mantel. When the hour struck, she wiped her hands on her apron and slowly took it off.

"Is dinner ready?" Connor asked from where he sat in a heavy chair near the fire.

"Connor Jessup, there's something I need to tell you."

Connor leaned forward, his expression closed. "What is it?"

"I'm leaving you." She wiped at her nose with the back of her hand. "Dinner's in the pot."

"What do you mean, you're leaving me?" He studied her for a moment before continuing. "Running off with that silver miner, aren't you?"

Elizabeth looked away.

"That's it, isn't it?" He stood and walked over to a rough-sawn cedar cupboard. Throwing the door open, he grabbed a glass bottle filled with light brown liquid. He returned to his chair and plopped himself down, taking a long drink.

Elizabeth walked into another room and came back carrying a small bag. "This marriage is over. Take care, Connor," she called as she softly closed the door.

Connor ignored her and continued to drink, keeping his gaze focused on the fire. "You can't leave, Elizabeth. I still love you," he whispered long after she was gone.

Bethany opened her eyes and stared at the rough oiled fabric of her enclosure. So, Elizabeth left behind a husband when she traveled here. Perhaps this Connor Jessup held the answer to the woman's presence in Paran and the Plane of Keilah, and her possession of the Book of Eitel. But how was she going to find him?

Bethany emerged from the heavy-blanketed opening of her tent. It was still early and only a few of the workers had risen. Carefully, she made her way to the stream that ran at the foot of their camp. Fallen branches made up a series of steps, helping her keep her footing on the muddy bank.

Once reaching the water, she turned to face the north and kneeled down. Raising her arms to the sky, she began to pray, "Mother of All, hold me safe in the palm of your hand. Bring me inner peace. Teach me tolerance of others. Teach me self-less love. Dear Mother, guide me on the path of enlightenment." Bethany lowered her arms and touched her forehead to the water. Standing, she brushed the dirt from her knees and started to walk along the edge of the stream. She pulled the hair comb out of the soft leather pouch she wore around her waist and ran her fingers over it. Again and again, she caressed the tortoise shell and its carvings.

She froze. In her mind's eye, she saw Elizabeth Jessup once more. Elizabeth was standing in a cave, but it wasn't a kiyolo. It was different somehow, with heavy timbers bracing the sides and ceiling. The man Bethany saw arriving in Paran with Elizabeth handed her the same silver box Ian had found yesterday.

"One of the men came across it when he was digging last night," he commented, turning it over in his hand. "Strange, it looks like silver, but it's not Nevada silver. The patina's too dark." He shook the box. "Some sort of book is in here, but I can't read the writing. Must be foreign or something."

Elizabeth eyed the box possessively. "You are going to give it to me aren't you, Michael?" Her voice was a soft caress.

Michael smiled. "You are a greedy one, Lizzy. Of course, that's something I always admired about you." He handed the box over to her outstretched hands. "I went looking for the workman who found it, to see if there were any more treasures to be had." He shook his head. "He was stone cold dead when I found him. Doc said it was his heart."

"Peace to you today, Bethany."

Bethany stared straight through Ian as he approached her, trying to make some sense of what she had just seen.

"Are you all right?"

"Y-yes. Of course. I'm fine." She blinked her eyes hard, clearing her sight. "Are you ready to head for Paran?"

"The wagon's loaded." Ian bent his tall frame down near the stream and splashed cold water over his face. It ran down his auburn hair and stained his bright red tunic. "We're just waiting for you."

The pair worked their way back up the side of the embankment to where the wagon was held. Two dohas, large four-legged temperamental animals with thick muscles and even thicker fur, were harnessed to the front end with one of the workers, Thomas, astride the largest of the two animal's backs. With one hand, he held onto the steering rein; the other hand was wrapped tight around the doha's long, coarse black fur.

"You had better get a move on, I don't know how much longer I can hold her steady!" Thomas called out as he spotted Ian and Bethany.

They hurried to the back of the vehicle. Ian started to offer Bethany a hand, but she had already situated herself on the padded seat. Ian sighed and took his seat on the opposite bench. "You don't always have to be so independent, you know."

Bethany looked at Ian as if she only now noticed his presence. *You'd think I was eight instead of twenty-eight.* "You really should be used to me by now, Ian." She rose up in her seat for a moment and called to the driver. "We're ready, Thomas!"

With a sudden jerk that sent her back into her seat, the dohas began to push the massive bones of their bodies in unison, pulling the heavy wheeled wood wagon behind them. Since the Digger's site was located only half a sun's ride from the town, they would arrive there by the mid-day meal.

Bethany leaned over, resting her arms across her legs. Absently, she rolled the hem of her patchwork blouse between thumb and forefinger, thinking of the vision she'd had at the stream.

"So, tell me, Beth," Ian interrupted her thoughts, "have you come up with any more details about the box?"

"If you mean have I been in the Knowing yet today, no I haven't," she answered, a little more sharply than she had intended. She shifted on the bench, trying to gain some measure of comfort. The road was well laid with smooth heavy stones, but the stride of the dohas was jerky and unpredictable and caused the large cart to lurch with a strange rhythm. Her stomach cramped, and she knew it was nearing the time for her menses. That alone made her reconsider the possibility of taking Ian as a lover, as the act of love helped ease the pain of a woman's monthly cycle. She looked at him. The wide brimmed hat he wore shadowed his light blue eyes. She had probably hurt his feelings by answering so harshly, though he'd never admit it. He pampered her too much. She wanted to be left to do what she wanted, whether it was traveling with the Diggers or staying home with Sarah.

"I'm sorry I spoke so rudely, Ian."

"That's all right."

She leaned against the back of the bench. For as long as she could remember, once her gift as a Knower revealed itself, everyone expected her to always be in the Knowing. *They'll never understand the mental and physical toll it takes.*

"You know I only go there when I need to or when my job with the expedition requires it. It's not a constant state I care to live in. I prefer to stay grounded."

Just then, a low tree branch came up behind Ian and knocked his hat free before Bethany had a chance to warn him. She started laughing as he made a grab for it, catching it just before it flew out of his reach. The laughter was exactly what she needed to ease her nerves. "Oh, Ian, this find has me on edge. I'm seeing things without being in the Knowing. I'm not used to that."

Ian glanced up. "Tell me what you've seen. Perhaps I can help make some sense of it."

"Not yet. I need some more time with my thoughts before I try to interpret them for you. For anyone." *Including myself.*

Bethany looked out over the hilly countryside. She thought of her child, and the girl's love of the outdoors. "I really miss Sarah. You know, I've been thinking. I want to bring her back with us after this visit."

"A site's not the place for children. There's too much trouble she could get into."

Bethany bristled. "Sarah is well behaved, Ian. She wouldn't be any trouble. Besides, she's seven now and I need to begin teaching her how to use the Knowing, as well as how to heal."

Ian took a deep breath and let it out slowly. Bethany felt him fighting something inside himself. Anger, perhaps. She couldn't be sure, as Ian wasn't one to show his temper. "All right, Bethany," he conceded. "Whatever you want."

THE SUN WAS high in its path when the wagon approached Paran. Bethany leaned forward, looking past Ian, watching for her home. Sure enough, not too far from where they were, she spied the small, flat stone structure. Sitting on the front stoop was Father. Thomas called the dohas to a halt and, before either he or Ian could disembark, Bethany was rushing down the side of the vehicle. Quickly, she stepped onto the rim of the wheel, then the spoke. She landed with a splash as her boot hit a mud puddle. Laughing, she ran the rest of the way home, her blonde hair blazing behind her.

Then, just as quickly, she pulled up short as she saw what her father was doing. In front of him, he held the wooden effigy of a small child. Bethany's heart leapt, thinking of the pain suffered by the parents of one so young.

Abraham Stendi was a carver of totems. When a person died, the family commissioned him to forever capture the form so those still alive would not forget them. These figures were used as structural members of the people's houses. Often, an adult's form replaced a post that had held up the roof. A child's might flank the fireplace. This would remind them that though a loved one was dead in body, their spirit still remained nearby.

"Oh, Papa, not a child." She dropped to her knees beside him. This was the hardest of all totems for him to carve. Abraham's deeply creased face appeared even older this day, the bright sunlight accentuating the wrinkles.

Abraham didn't hear or see his daughter. He only murmured some unintelligible words.

"Papa? I can't understand what you're saying." She glanced around, the sun hurting her eyes. A sense of foreboding filled her. "Papa, where's Sarah?"

"My poor, poor baby."

A chill ran through Bethany. Ian walked up behind her and put his hand on her shoulder. "What's going on, Beth?"

"I don't know." She looked closer at the totem and her stomach lurched. Bethany wrested the carving from her father's hands. No. It couldn't be.

"*Sarah!*"

CHAPTER THREE

"Tell me what happened. Papa, where's my daughter?"

Abraham sat on his heels and rocked back and forth. Bethany grabbed him by the upper arms and forced him to look into her face.

"Bethany. You've come home," he whispered.

Bethany swallowed hard, fighting the wave of panic that threatened her composure. Surely there was a reasonable explanation for the totem. Maybe it was another child that just happened to look like her Sarah.

"Where is she? Where's Sarah?" She gently shook him. "Tell me, Papa. Why are you making this totem? Who's it for?"

"Can't you tell? It's our baby." He looked down at his hands. "Am I so old and inept you can't make out my carvings anymore?"

Bethany fell backward against Ian's legs. He caught her and, stooping down, held her close against his chest. "What happened, Abraham?"

"Don't know. Don't know. She was playing outside, then she was gone." He rubbed his eyes hard with the backs of his swollen knuckles. "Gone, like a butterfly. I think she flew away. So pretty. So pretty. I knew this would happen someday. The Mother Goddess wanted her for her own."

Bethany looked at her father, tears clouding her vision. "No." She pivoted around, and her eyes met Ian's. "*No!*" she screamed and wrenched herself free of his embrace. Jumping to her feet, she ran into the woods near the dwelling. "Sarah!" she screamed. "Sarah! It's Momma! Come to me baby!" The only sound that answered was her own voice, echoing off the stony mountains in the distance.

"I'm FIXING you some bitters. It'll help you to sleep," Ian said.

Bethany stared at him through red, teary eyes. "You can't be serious," she whispered. "I won't sleep until I know where my daughter is."

Ian stoked the fire, heating the orange flavored bitters until it steamed. "This should calm you. You'll be no good to anyone if you're not rested."

"I don't need rest. I need answers," she answered bluntly. Rising, she walked over to the fire and picked up the iron tongs. She used them to turn over a log, then hung them back on their hook. Simple tasks were all she could handle right now.

Bethany sat back down, letting her gaze drift about the room. From the heavily beamed open ceiling hung the dried herbs she and Sarah had gathered during the season of harvest, the hottest months of the year. Next to the wide planked wood door sat Sarah's small doll, one she'd had since she was a baby. She picked it up and cradled it close; the clothes were well worn and the doll threadbare from so many washings, from being loved so well. Everywhere she looked, she saw her daughter and sensed her presence.

"Papa, I have to know what happened," she pleaded, turning her attention to Abraham. "Tell me."

"I know, I know you want me to explain but I don't know. I don't remember. She was here one moment and then... she was gone." He wrung his hands together, his eyes darting back and forth between Bethany and the fire. "What'll we do without her? She's my sun."

Bethany took a deep breath, steadying her nerves, then placed her left hand in the center of Abraham's back. "I'm going to help you remember, Papa."

He pulled away from her touch. "No! I don't want to remember. It'll hurt too much. She's gone. She's gone." He shook his head and moaned. "That's all there is to know, Daughter. Truly, it is. Let the butterfly be."

She placed her hands on his face and turned him to face her. His eyes shone with the crazed light of someone who hadn't slept in days. As she continued to stare at him, she felt the subtle vibration that happened when her eyes turned from their natural topaz to clear azure. The fire penetrated her and she drew from its strength. A fine layer of sweat covered her body.

Bethany applied pressure to Abraham's back with her left hand; with her right, she kneaded his solar plexus. She saw the multi-hued colors of his aura and sought to repair the tears to the green heart center by the trauma of his granddaughter's disappearance. The tears and gashes in the very fabric of his energy were deep and filled with panic and fear. She continued to focus on making them whole, closing the openings, drawing out the poison of the pain. As the wounds closed, and he became whole once more, she closed her eyes and let her hands drop.

Abraham gasped and fell forward, his head barely missing the raised hearth. Ian rushed to his side and helped him to his chair. "Are you all right, Beth?" he asked as he helped the older man settle.

Bethany didn't answer. She clutched the cup of now cooled bitters and downed it in one long drink. She tried to put the vessel back on the table, but her hands shook so violently, Ian had to take it from her.

"I remember now, Daughter," Abraham whispered.

Bethany closed her eyes, bracing herself. "Tell me."

"Four days ago, I was working in the yard, cleaning up wood shavings. I had just finished a totem for the Krueg clan. Their grandmother, Maryl, died the last night of the Red Moon." Abraham's voice was low and raspy. Ian poured him a cup of the hot drink. Abraham nodded his thanks and took a small sip.

He continued, "Sarah was playing near the trees. I said, 'Don't go near those woods, girl. The Eitellans'll get you.' "

Bethany shivered upon hearing the old warning. "Then what?"

"You know your daughter, Bethany." He shook his head. "She's as stubborn as you are. I went inside for a moment and when I came out, she was gone. I assumed she had gone to play at Herran's. You know how inseparable those two girls are."

He smiled for a moment, lost in a memory. "Well, when she didn't come home that evening, I went to Herran's house. They hadn't seen Bethany all day. After that, I went to every door in Paran, looking for the child. The next morning, I found this about a half a mile into the woods." He reached into his pocket and pulled out a bright yellow hair ribbon. "She was wearing it that day," Abraham said, his voice breaking. He held the ribbon to his nose as if to inhale her fragrance. It caught the tears as they streamed down the old man's cheek.

Bethany reached out her hand and Abraham placed the damp ribbon ever so gently into her palm. Bethany clutched it to her breast.

"Beth, are you sure you should be doing this? Perhaps we ought to find someone else," Ian offered.

"No, Ian. I'll do it myself. I have to know what happened." She braced herself as the familiar vibration filled her and she slipped into the Knowing.

CHAPTER FOUR

Sarah, so bright and full of life, was dressed in her favorite pink tunic and knee high tan boots. She ran, dodging the tall conifer trunks, chasing a small rodent. Her laughter filled the air like the sound of tinkling wind chimes. Bethany smiled. The furry animal scurried under a fallen log. Sarah climbed on top of it.

"Please, little friend, come out and play some more," she begged, leaning over. Then, as if sensing another's presence, Sarah straightened and turned around. A short, squat woman dressed in a dark flowing robe approached.

"My, my. What have we here?" the woman asked.

Sarah took a step backward and stumbled off the log. The woman moved as fast as her bulk would allow. She caught Sarah by the hand and pulled her upright. Sarah laughed and curtsied. She slipped and started to fall again, but managed to regain her balance. "Who are you?" she asked, her eyes wide.

"Why, I'm Esther, little one."

"Do you live in the woods? I've heard stories about people who live with the trees. Do you turn into a tree at night?"

"So many questions!" Esther chuckled. "I live hereabouts," she said, her arm moving in a wide sweeping motion. "And no, I do not turn into a tree. That's just pretend." She smiled, taking a step closer to Sarah. "Would you like to come and play with me today? I have a friend who'd love to meet you."

Sarah hesitated for a moment. "If I do, I need to first ask my Grandfather if it's all right to visit with you. I'm not supposed to wander off. Everyone says the Eitellans will get me if I do."

"Oh, now, I know your grandfather very well. We won't be gone too long and I promise to have you home for the evening meal and I'll take him a loaf of my fresh baked bread. Is that all right with you?"

"Well, I guess so." Sarah shrugged her shoulders and jumped down from the log. She took hold of Esther's hand.

"Have you ever met a real priestess before?" Esther asked.

Sarah shook her head and, as she did so, the ribbon slipped out of her hair and fell to the ground.

Bethany exhaled, not realizing she had been holding her breath. "Oh, Papa," she whispered. She laid her head down, resting it on her arms. Her body shuddered, wracked with deep sobs.

"What did you see, Beth?" Ian asked, his voice quiet and gentle.

She shook her head. Ian placed one hand on her shoulder; with the other, he caressed her cheek. "Please, let me help you. You know I care about you and Sarah."

She sniffed and blinked hard, fighting to control the tears. "A short heavy-set woman took her away. The woman–*Esther*–she wore a dark robe." She struggled with the memory and what it meant. "She mentioned something about a priestess."

"A priestess! But there've been no priestess cults since...since..."

Bethany finished the sentence for him. "Since the Eitellans."

BETHANY PACED the floor of the small house while Abraham and Ian slept. The heavy planks groaned their protests as she passed in front of the hearth. Her sadness embedded itself into her bones and wouldn't let her rest.

Over and over, she replayed the scene of Sarah's encounter in the woods. Could all of this be connected? First, the discovery of what appeared to be the Book of Eitel, then, Sarah's disappearance in the forest—to meet a priestess. Were any other children missing? According to legend if so, did it mean the re-emergence of the Eitellans? Come first light she would find out if more children were missing. She would also seek out a Weaver to help her make sense of the stories, and her visions of Elizabeth Jessup.

ABRAHAM ROSE EARLY, as he usually did. In his old age, he rarely needed much sleep. He found his daughter slumped over in a chair near the fire, asleep. Her hair, like a golden curtain, brushed against the floor. He walked over and pushed it away from her face. She stirred. "Peace to you, my child."

"Peace to you, Father," she murmured, rubbing the sleep from her eyes.

Abraham grunted as he settled himself into the chair opposite hers at the table. "Have you slept much?"

"Not really. The visions won't let me." She picked up the pitcher of bitters from the night before. It was stone cold, but she didn't care. She poured a cupful and took a sip. She shivered as the drink made its way to her stomach, feeling the coldness move throughout her. "Do you know if there are other children missing from here, Father?"

"Well, now that you mention it, I haven't seen any of the little beggars lately. You know, the ones who stay near the square looking for handouts? People were saying they probably wandered off into the woods, but they've been gone for quite some time. And they always come back, especially with winter approaching." He shook his head sadly, dropping his chin to his chest. "I didn't think of it when Sarah disappeared. So many babes."

Bethany's stomach dropped, her worst fears realized. But how do you fight against what you don't understand? "I need to find a Weaver, Papa, to help me understand the old legends of the Eitel. Do you know any who might still carry those stories with them? It seems a dying knack."

He poured himself a cup of the cold beverage and sipped, deep in thought. He drummed his fingers against the tabletop. "Yes, actually. There's one who lives down by the river. Her name's Maud Hekate. Now that I think about it, she stopped by last winter, on her way to town. She was looking for someone to apprentice so her stories wouldn't be lost." He rose and began to walk toward the front door. "I don't know what's happened to my mind. I should've remembered that."

"Where are you going, Father?" Bethany asked.

He turned around and looked at her curiously. "Why, to find the Weaver."

Bethany stood. "Please stay here, in case Sarah returns." Though as she said it, she knew it wouldn't happen. But she couldn't bear it if something happened to him as well.

"Oh. Yes. Of course, Daughter, I'll wait here. You'll send for me if you need my help?"

She hugged him tight then kissed his cheek. "I will."

BETHANY SLIPPED FROM THE HOUSE, leaving Ian dozing in a padded chair and her father sorting wood into piles on the front stoop. She made her way down a path at the far end of their land and headed for the river. The water wasn't far, maybe only a quarter day's walk, and it felt good to Bethany to move. She picked up the pace to a trot and wound her way through the path between the trees.

This is what she needed. To stretch her body and work out the pain, to let what she'd seen in the Knowing settle so she could make sense of it.

Her mind cleared and she felt a renewed hope, filling her like the pine scent that surrounded the forest. *I will find you, Sarah.*

Approaching the riverbank, Bethany scanned up and down, looking for the Weaver's dwelling place. Then, she spotted it; about midway across to the other side was a small island with a mud hut situated at its center. Bethany waded into the river and swam toward the land. Her clothing, wet and heavy against her skin, slowed her progress. She stopped and treaded for a moment, catching her breath.

Suddenly, a stone splashed near her head. She looked up abruptly. An old woman stood on the island's shore, getting ready to toss another rock. Bethany ducked under the water and resurfaced about five feet away just as it came her way. "Stop!" she yelled. "I'm not going to hurt you!"

"Go away!" the woman spat back. "I don't want any visitors." She threw a stick, then went back inside her hut, slamming the door behind her. Bethany continued to swim in the island's direction, ignoring the warning.

The old one has been alone too long, the solitude has affected her mind.

Reaching the shore, Bethany rung her hair and clothing out as best as she could, shivering at the chill. She stepped onto the wooden stoop and knocked on the door.

"I told you to go away," came the muffled voice from within.

"Please, I need to speak to a woman named, Maud Hekate. Are you Maud?" Bethany called through the moss-covered wood.

The door flung open, almost knocking Bethany off her feet. The old woman stood in the doorway, her stooped shoulders draped in a blanket. Her long gray hair was matted and full of twigs. "What if I am? What's it to you?"

"I have need of a Weaver," Bethany explained.

"Too bad. Go away." Maud started to pull the door closed, but Bethany grabbed it and forced it open.

"I won't go away until you tell me the old stories of Eitel."

The old woman retreated slightly. "I don't tell those stories to just anyone, you know."

Bethany sighed. "I'm sure you don't, but I'd like to ask you to make an exception. I could pay," she offered.

Maud snorted at first then her eyes narrowed as she looked past Bethany's shoulder.

Bethany turned around. All she could see was a pile of soggy driftwood near the water's shore. It was covered with seaweed and the remains of barnacles that the birds had missed. She turned back to Maud. "Well?"

"Hmmph, you certainly can't come into my home dripping water everywhere, now can you? You see that pile of wood?"

Bethany nodded.

"It needs to be dried out for firewood. Take each piece and lay it flat behind the house where the sun's sure to hit it. When you're done you should be good and dry. Come see me then." She sniffed. "Maybe we'll talk."

Bethany straightened. "I don't have time for this, Maud. I need answers right away."

Maud waved her hand as she entered the hut. "Don't we all, child. Don't we all." She closed the door behind her.

Bethany stood with her hands on her hips, staring after the old woman. She checked the sun's path. It was almost noon. Well, it looked like Maud wasn't going to come back out until the work was done.

She took a deep breath and walked over to the woodpile. It was at least a foot taller than she was. Unable to reach the top, Bethany decided to pull a log out from the middle. This was her first mistake as everything started to tumble down, part of it splashing into the water. Bethany kicked at a branch in frustration, yelping when it hurt her toe.

Enough! Pay the price so you can hear about Eitel.

Leaning over, she began to gather the smaller logs into her arms and tote them to the area Maud had indicated. As the sun approached the horizon, Bethany had finally finished.

She was sitting on the front stoop, catching her breath, when Maud walked out. "So, I see you're done."

"Did you think I wouldn't finish?" Bethany asked.

"Oh, I knew you would, *if* you wanted to know the stories bad enough, that is."

"Are you saying I had to do this to prove I really wanted to hear about Eitel?"

"Uh-huh, that's exactly what I'm saying." She stood. "Well, what are you waiting for?" She turned around and walked back into the hut. "Come on in."

The opening was small, and Bethany had to duck to pass through the entry. Once inside, her senses were assaulted with the smell of soured meat and bitters. She looked around and found a small armless chair near the fire. She waited until Maud was settled, then sat down opposite her.

"Eitel, you say?" Maud asked quietly. "I haven't had to weave those stories in a long time. No one cares much any more about them. Why do you want to know?"

"My daughter is missing. She was taken to see a priestess."

"A priestess! Do you know that for certain?" The old woman's eyes glistened in the firelight.

"I'm a Knower. I've seen the vision," Bethany stated simply.

Maud nodded slowly. "I should've guessed." She closed her light-colored eyes and when she opened them, they were a bright blue. Bethany caught her breath. Maud was a Knower too!

"Why has a Knower become a Weaver?" Bethany asked quietly.

"The same reason a Knower becomes a Healer. To give us the opportunity to concentrate on something else outside of ourselves."

The woman had read her. Bethany nodded in understanding. No one could be in the Knowing all the time as the sights would drive them crazy. They needed a distraction from their own minds.

Maud raised her hands in front of her and slowly strummed her fingers against the air. Dimly lit sparks formed, becoming long, thin lines of light, forming a warp. Once the warp had fully manifested, she started working on the weft. Bright, colorful lines emerged from her fingers as her hands moved in graceful swirls in the air.

"Hundreds of years ago, there lived a simple man, a man called Eitel. His aspirations were not great until the day a visitor from another plane approached him, a woman called Yongi. She was an evil priestess and sought to expand her power. Yongi fell in love with Eitel and shared her magic with him, making him all-powerful—a god.

"She lured women to serve as his priestesses under her. She was the first High Priestess."

Bethany sat transfixed as the strands became brighter and more colorful with the telling of the tale. Red, blue, green, the weaving began to resemble a cloth made from multi-colored fabric. The fabric of light continued to expand as Maud continued to pass her hands over the illuminated strands.

"A scribe among them put Yongi's magic words to paper and created the Book of Eitel. When the task was complete, the man was killed to insure his silence. This book contains the secrets of their cult. The secrets of traveling between the planes. The secrets of immortality." Maud paused, taking a deep breath. The cloth was almost complete. "But it is said only the high priestess can live forever and she must do this through the sacrifice of others. She seeks children and drains the very souls from their bodies, absorbing all the years of life they had ahead of them."

"Do the children die then?"

"No, according to legend, they only die if the forms are not cared for properly. They enter a state of perpetual sleep. It is in the priestess's best interests to see the bodies cared for, for if one of them deteriorated she would lose that soul and its years."

Bethany leaned forward. "Can the priestess be stopped?"

"The legends say she can be killed…" Her eyes narrowed as she continued to weave. "I am sorry, they do not reveal how it can be done. It will be up to you to discover the truth on your journey."

"Do you know any stories of travelers from the Earth plane?"

Maud's eyes widened. Her hands fell to her sides and the illuminated fabric burst into flames and disappeared. Maud's gaze locked with Bethany's. "Why do you ask?"

"In my vision, I saw a woman. She came from Earth and carried the Book of Eitel with her. I have the box she brought, with the manuscript, but no key. I read the container and found out that whoever forces the lock will die." Bethany took hold of Maud's hands to show her what her vision had been but instead she saw a glimpse into the old one's past…

There, in the darkness of her mind, she saw Maud as a child, walking between a young couple, her hands clasped in theirs. Maud and the woman were wearing matching bright dresses made of a soft light blue fabric, decorated with tiny yellow flowers. The young man wore trousers with a crisp white shirt and suspenders, a hat at a jaunty angle on his head. They strolled along the side of a mountain, smiling and singing as they walked.

With a gasp, Bethany let go of Maud's hands. "You're from Earth!" she exclaimed. "I wasn't sure it was possible."

"Of course it's possible, if you know the secrets." Maud chuckled. "But, I'm not truly an Earth being. It was my mother who crossed the planes. I'm part of Earth and part of Keilah, as my father is from Paran."

"How do I get there? I need to seek out the traveler's husband and find what he knows of her connection to Eitel."

"Why haven't you looked for the traveler herself?" Maud asked.

"I believe she's dead. I saw flames shooting up around the woman and the man who followed her in my vision. And there was a great deal of ash and bone fragments at the Digger site where I was working and the book was found." Bethany shivered.

"Hmm, I see." Maud was silent for a moment. "Well, it's a dangerous journey to the Earth plane but, as one Knower to another, I won't try to stop you. Whatever I tell you, though, you must not repeat. Not everyone is suited for traveling in such a way."

"Agreed."

"Good. Now, do you know the stories of the portal?" Maud asked.

Bethany nodded. "Some."

"Travel to the mountains in the north. There, you'll find a sheer wall of solid stone. Look closely for a break about a hand's breadth wide." Maud held up her hand sideways. "Look closer still and you'll also see a blue glow. Call out to the Keeper for permission to enter. His name is Zachariah."

"He will let me pass?"

Maud shrugged. "Only if it suits him."

Bethany rose to leave. "Thank you for sharing your stories with me, Maud." She reached into her waist pouch and extracted a small gold ingot. She pressed it into Maud's palm. "Peace to you, Sister."

Bethany left the hut and took a deep cleansing breath. "Zachariah will let me pass," she whispered. "He has to."

CHAPTER FIVE

As the moon reached its apex in the night sky, Bethany emerged from her resting place in the hollow of a tree and began her journey north. Not wanting to draw undue attention from anyone who might be nearby, she paused for a moment and bound her golden tresses tightly to her head lest they attract the moon's glow. She reached into her pouch and extracted a long wooden pin, fastening the knot in place.

A breeze swirled around her, and the small hollow bones in her earrings caught the wind and whistled. It was a low, primeval moan, carrying the song of the soul.

She shivered and hugged her arms tightly about her as she walked, pulling her shawl close.

Winter will soon be here… I must find Sarah before the ice storms start.

Once the ice came, the people of Paran would be house-bound because of the dangerous shards that fell from the sky.

Bethany made her way through rough terrain, crowded by giant conifers and jagged rocks until she arrived at a clearing in the midst of it all. Able to see the sky, she looked up and surveyed the stars. Though they were beginning to fade with the rising of the sun, their position told her she wasn't far from her destination. Finally, at full light, she reached the mountains.

As Bethany continued northward, the landscape changed drastically. The tall conifers disappeared, replaced with low, dense brush. Already, the heavy frosts that preceded the ice storms had started to kill the foliage, turning it a rusty brown. The rocks grew in size the farther she traveled, impeding her progress.

As she climbed over a boulder, something caught her eye. She stopped and examined the flat wall of shale before her. A soft blue glow emanated from a crack in the side of the mountain, just as Maud said it would. Bethany leapt down from the boulder and approached the opening cautiously.

"Who are you?" a loud voice bellowed from within the stone.

So the stories were true! There really was a Keeper. And a portal. She fought to steady her nerves. "I am Bethany M'Doro, Sir."

"What is it you seek, Bethany M'Doro?"

"Zachariah, the Keeper of the Portal."

"If it's your fortune you want told, he's not working today. Don't waste your time here. Leave now."

Of course, she should have expected this. The legends said the Keeper was able to reveal the future. "I don't seek a reading, Sir, nor am I going anywhere until I talk to Zachariah himself."

Bethany stood her ground, waiting for a reply. After several moments, the stones started to shake. She took a step backward, her eyes wide. Slowly, the crevice in the mountain opened, a loud scraping sound filled the air. Behind the wall of rock, a floating mass of color was revealed—milky opal, filled with fiery bursts of color. She waited until the opening was wide enough to slip through then, bracing herself, entered the portal. As she walked, a deep vibration shook her body.

Once through the opal fog, Bethany struggled to gain her footing. She took a step forward and reached a large window, blinking against the brightness that emanated from the other side. Here, in the world between the planes, two suns rotated around each other filling the sky almost completely with their light.

"Come away from the window, you," a voice called impatiently from behind her. "Those mortal eyes of yours will burn out if you stay there staring like that."

"It's so beautiful," she whispered, turning away from the light. As she did so, her vision filled with the sight of a huge pyramid-shaped hall, hewn from the solid rock. Here and there were paintings encrusted with multi-colored gems set into the stone walls. The wind that passed from her world to this one swirled around her feet, tugging at the bottom of her heavy cotton leggings.

"Mmm. I suppose, but it is within this beauty that lies the danger. Allow yourself to become entangled in the spell those suns cast and you'll live the remainder of your life a slave." The man turned around to face Bethany squarely. "A slave to darkness."

Bethany took a step backward as her stomach lurched. The man's eyes were as milky white as the portal she had just crossed. "I see you must speak from experience, Sir."

"So it would seem." The man laughed, the deep rattling sound echoing through the chamber. "So it would seem."

"Are you Zachariah?" Bethany asked. The man before her didn't quite fit her image of what a Keeper should look like with his bald head and long white mustache. But then, she didn't really have a point of reference.

"I am." He motioned with his hand toward a pair of gilt chairs positioned before a great fireplace. "Sit with me."

Bethany obliged nervously, waiting until Zachariah had taken his place before sitting down. When she did, the soft red and purple velvet cushions molded around her body. After walking for so many hours she was exhausted. The muscles in her legs tightened and cramped. She gasped and had to massage her thighs to lessen the ache.

She leaned against the high back of the chair, focusing on Zachariah. Around his body hovered what seemed dust motes of varying colors.

The shades of life.

The outermost ring was composed of light blue particles, followed by indigo and, finally, deep purple. The colors reflected his great knowledge and deep spirituality.

"I need your help, Zachariah," she began.

"As does everyone who crosses the portal." He sighed and shook his head wearily. "But then, you did say you didn't want to know your fortune, didn't you?" He cocked his head toward her, waiting for a response.

She nodded and her earrings chimed together. "I wish to travel to the Earth plane. I seek answers to my daughter's disappearance."

Zachariah snorted. "What makes you think they can be found there? Many have sought to journey and return disappointed.

Bethany shifted in her chair. There wasn't time for lengthy explanations, but she forced herself to calmly speak of her need. "I believe my child was taken by the Eitellans. The Eitellans are—"

"I know who the Eitellans are, Bethany M'Doro. Don't belabor your story," Zachariah interrupted.

She eyed the man intently before continuing. "I don't appreciate your rudeness, Sir. I was merely trying to tell you the sequence of events that brought me here. My daughter Sarah has disappeared. My only clue in finding her at this time is a man from the Earth plane, Connor Jessup." She crossed her arms against her chest. "Was that brief enough for you?"

Zachariah chuckled. "You do have fire, girl. I'll give you that. No one has addressed me in such a tone in a long time. I must say I find it quite refreshing."

Bethany took a deep breath and let it out slowly. Good. She hadn't angered him. "So, will you let me pass?"

"Not so fast. First, we'll need to see what we can find out about this Connor Jessup. You just can't go running across the planes without any kind of direction, you know!" He twirled the long hairs of his mustache thoughtfully. "And, there's the matter of payment."

"Payment?" Bethany echoed.

"You didn't think I'd let you pass without some kind of retribution, did you?"

"No, no. Of course not," Bethany murmured. "I have modest means, but I'll try to pay whatever you demand."

"There now. That's what I like to hear. But, what could you give me that I don't already have? I don't need food or gold." He smiled slyly. "I know! I think I'll take one of those eyes of yours."

Bethany jumped to her feet. "My eye? You can't be serious."

"Oh, I'm quite serious. It's the only thing I really need at this point in my life. Mark my words, though." He shook his fist toward the window. The ruby ring he wore glinted in the light, casting a red beam onto the smooth stone floor. "This time I'll not let those blasted suns ruin it."

"You really mean it." Bethany fell back into the chair. She closed first one eye, then the other, trying to imagine a world with single vision.

Would the loss affect the Knowing?

It didn't really matter, though. Had she been asked, she'd gladly have given her life to save Sarah's. If an eye was the price of passage, she would pay it.

"All right, Zachariah. I'll give what you ask of me."

Zachariah tilted his head to one side. If he had been able to see, Bethany would have guessed he was considering her sincerity. She shifted uncomfortably, needing to be on her way. Every moment delayed meant that much longer before she would be able to help Sarah.

"I said I'd give you an eye, Zachariah. But there's something I must tell you." She leaned forward. "I'm a Knower and there's a chance this power may be transferred with the eye. You may get more than you bargained for."

Zachariah waved his hand. "None of that matters to me. The chance to see this world of mine again is all I want." He stood slowly and motioned for her to come nearer. "I grow weary of this chatter. Here. Stand directly in front of me." He took hold of her shoulders and steadied her. Placing his hands on either side of her face, he felt a slight dampness.

"What's this? Crying are we?"

"Please, it doesn't really matter, does it?" Bethany's mind was in a whirl. She wondered again what life would be like with only single sight. Would the extraction be painful? She cringed. For a brief moment, vanity overcame her. What would she look like? Would children run from the one-eyed woman? Bethany took a deep breath and pushed the thoughts away. "I'm ready. Take the eye."

"Close them, then."

Bethany looked at the man, taken aback. "How can you take it if my eyes are closed?"

"It's a simple magical process I use. The transference will take place quickly and painlessly. Well, almost painlessly. Now, do as I say."

She complied. So much in her world was beyond belief these days, why should she question this? Zachariah moved his hands from the sides of her face. His fingers traced the lines of her profile— the pert nose, full lips, and wide set eyes. "I'll bet you're considered quite lovely in your world, aren't you?"

Bethany found it impossible to answer as she steeled herself against the pain Zachariah spoke of.

"And so serious, I see." Zachariah moved his hands again, placing an index finger over each eye. "Let's see. Which one shall I take?"

"Take whichever one pleases you the most. It doesn't matter to me. Just do it now!"

Zachariah paused for a moment, then deposited a light kiss on her forehead. He lowered his hands. "There now, that didn't hurt too much, did it?"

Bethany stood frozen. Actually, it hadn't hurt at all. She slowly opened her eyes. The room came into complete focus. "Zachariah, what's going on here? I can still see perfectly."

He laughed. "Of course, you can. What use would I have for sight at my age? There's nothing left that I haven't already seen." He shuffled over to his seat near the fire and sat down. Bethany was fast on his heels.

"Why did you put me through that? Is this how you amuse yourself?"

Zachariah leaned forward, his face serious. "Listen to me, Bethany M'Doro. What just happened was neither for my pleasure nor for your agony. It was a test."

"A test?" she repeated quietly, sinking into her chair.

"Of course. Do you think I grant passage to just anyone? This is a serious thing, traveling between the planes. I had to be certain of your commitment to your goal. If you would seek this man, Connor Jessup, then I will help you find him. There is one condition, though."

Bethany looked at the man warily. She'd had enough of his games. "What now?"

"You won't be allowed to cross over to Earth in the physical form."

"Why not?"

"Because you're too emotionally involved with this quest of yours. You could become locked into that plane with no hope of ever returning to Keilah. What good would you be to your daughter then?"

He stood and walked over to the window, his face toward the suns. "I will, however, permit you to travel as a shadow. Being a Knower, you should have no problem with this form of mental imagery."

"A shadow? I fail to see what good that will do me. I need to talk to the man and find out what he knows." She stood next to Zachariah and placed her hand on his arm. "Is there no other way?"

"Not for you, Bethany M'Doro. Not for you." He turned to face her. "But if you can draw him to the portal's entry in his world, I will allow him to cross over to this place, the same as I allowed you. You can talk to him here." He held out his hand. "We need to consult the Akashic Records to see exactly where–and when-this Connor Jessup exists."

CHAPTER SIX

Bethany followed Zachariah down a long winding corridor. The ceiling was high and vaulted and, though carved from the mountain, glowed with its own light. She looked closer, realizing the entire surface of the passageway was covered with a thin layer of gold. Bethany ran her hand along the wall as she walked, feeling the uneven texture of the plating against the rock.

"How did this place come to be?" she whispered.

"The portal was created by an ancient race of beings known as the Aztecs. They lived on the plane of Tectal and were often visited by travelers from other planes. These people came to admire the Aztec's great ability to form gold and jewels into almost any shape." He stopped walking just as they reached a junction in the passage. "Feel this." Zachariah ran his hand along the opening's casing. "Here's an example of what I mean."

"It's beautiful," Bethany breathed, touching the intricate carvings of panthers and gods, their eyes encrusted with cabochon emeralds and sapphires.

"The Aztec's contact with these people led them to understand the secrets of crossing from one realm to another. Eventually, they migrated to the Earth plane. During this time, they created the elaborate portal you're now visiting. One of them became the Keeper. All Keepers after are direct descendants as the duty is passed from parent to child."

"Do you have any children, Zachariah?"

Zachariah smiled. "I have a son. He is living on the plane of Satore and will return to take over when I die." He pointed down another hall. "Come, it's this way to the records."

Bethany gasped when she stepped over the threshold to the great hall of the Akashic Records. It contained the story of every person's life who ever existed from all the planes. "How long have the records been kept?" She turned in a slow circle as she took in the magnitude of the hall.

"Since the beginning of humankind." Zachariah shrugged his shoulders. "Give or take a few years."

The stacked towers of books stretched up as far as the eye could see and the hall continued well past her line of sight. "Will we be able to find Connor Jessup amongst all of this?" she asked.

Zachariah motioned for her to follow him. There, imbedded into the rock wall, was a flat clear window. Zachariah placed his hand in its center and a soft glow began to show from behind. Bethany thought she detected the smell of wildflowers emanating from the screen. He left his hand there for a moment longer. When he pulled it away, a slight impression remained on the glass.

"How is that possible?" Bethany asked, her eyes wide with wonder.

"It's how the crystal recognizes me, by reading the lines on my hand. You see, only the Keeper has access to this information. If you had tried to do the same, it would have remained solid."

He rubbed his chin and cleared his throat. "I seek the life of Connor Jessup of the Earth plane," he commanded in a deep voice.

A hum of sorts went up Bethany's spine and out through her limbs. And she felt, rather than heard, a voice reply... *Aisle fifteen, stack forty-two, volume ninety.*

She repeated the location aloud to the old man.

"You heard it?" he asked.

She nodded. "Yes, I did. At least, I felt something, and it told me where to look."

"A gift has been given to you, Bethany M'Doro. There have been few travelers who have heard a reply." He began to walk down the stacks. "A gift indeed. Truly, your mission will be blessed."

Bethany hurried to catch up with Zachariah as he breezed through one aisle after another. He muttered each number as he moved past stack after stack.

"Thirteen, fourteen, ah, here it is. Fifteen." He ran his hand along the spines of the volumes. "Stack forty-two. You'll need to climb the ladder and retrieve volume ninety."

She stared at the books before her. None of them were marked. "How am I to know which is number ninety?" she asked.

"You'll know."

Obliging him, she pulled the tall wooden ladder over from where it stood behind her, thankful that it was on wheels. Climbing one rung after another, she kept her eyes open for a sign. There it was! A book in the middle of the pile started to glow a deep red, where the others remained a midnight blue. "I found it. Now, how do I retrieve it without knocking everything down?"

"Just pull it out. Nothing will happen."

Bethany eyed Zachariah skeptically. "You mean to tell me I can remove this one book without sending the rest of them toppling down on top of us?"

"Still questioning, eh Bethany? I said it would be all right and it will be. Now, do you want to know about Connor Jessup or not?"

"Of course, I do." She gritted her teeth and gave the red book a good yank. To her amazement, it slid out easily. The balance of the manuscripts above it neatly lowered themselves into place. She climbed back down the ladder, shaking her head. "I swear I've seen everything now."

"Not quite, Bethany M'Doro. Your journey is just beginning."

ZACHARIAH LED Bethany to a small candle-lit reading area. There was only room enough for one to sit at the table so, out of respect, she was now standing, peering over his shoulder. She stared hard at the pages, trying to make some sense of the images before her.

"Here we are." Zachariah pointed with a long thin finger. "Connor Jessup."

"How can you tell? I mean, the writing makes no sense to me. And you can't see it." She glanced at him sideways. "Can you?"

"I can see it the same way the screen spoke to you. Its vibration flows into me and the pictures become clear in my head." He took her hand and pulled her around to the side of the table. Gently, he guided her fingers to the page. "You try it."

The moment Bethany touched the coarse paper, her mind exploded with images. A cabin set apart from a small town was nestled in the middle of dark, snow-covered mountains. The place and time came to her. *Devil's Gate, Nevada, 1875.*

The next image overlapped the first. A man asleep in bed, his breathing heavy and labored, a bottle sat beside him in bed. Somewhere outside a wolf howled and Bethany cringed, sensing the imminence of death. She pulled her hand away, shivering. "He's dying."

Zachariah nodded. "His time on Earth is almost over. According to the records, he transitions in 1875."

"I saw those numbers in my vision. I have to get to him, Zachariah, before he dies." Her voice was urgent. "Right now, he's my only link to finding Sarah."

"I understand." He stood. "Here, take my seat. Now, place both hands on the page of Connor Jessup's life and close your eyes."

Bethany did as she was instructed. Almost immediately she felt her energy shift, her body fading away from her consciousness. Suddenly, she was hovering above herself and Zachariah—disembodied. She looked down at her body and she appeared to be sleeping, her hands still on the book. She held her hands out in front of her and was surprised to find she could almost see right through them. *Is this real?* She glanced around, then realized she was floating, an almost imperceptible silver line running from her body to her shadow self. Zachariah tilted his head up, as if he were searching.

"Take care, Bethany," he murmured. "I'll give you two days to complete your journey. After that, you'll have to return here, or your body will cease to exist. You'll remain a shadow on the Earth plane forever."

CHAPTER SEVEN

"I understand," she answered, and the words were like the current of a river, flowing between them. "Where is the portal?" she asked.

"There." Zachariah pointed in the direction opposite from where he stood. "There is the crossing point to Earth."

Bethany tried to move, but her legs felt as heavy as stone.

Of course!

The answer came to her. The shadow state must be similar to the Knowing. Whenever she wanted to move at that time, all she had to do was clear her mind and think directly of the action she wished to perform. She tried it and, sure enough, it worked. Almost effortlessly she glided along the aisles formed by the records until she reached another portal. She hesitated just short of the opening.

"Dear Mother of All," she prayed. "Guide me safely on my journey and help me find all that I seek." Taking a deep breath, she passed through the entry.

Once through the continuum, she discovered a sky as dark as the deepest black onyx. Beneath it was a grid of brightly colored lines of light. The lines represented the different planes of existence in the universe. Along each one, millions of sparks traveled, echoing the essences of the beings living in that plane. Here and there, a spark would grow brighter then disintegrate.

That must be what death looks like…

Bethany struggled to see beyond the black horizon where the beams stretched off into oblivion. How was she going to find the Earth plane among all of these? But the instant she thought of Earth, one of the lines flashed. She thought of Earth again, holding the name in her mind and the color of the cable intensified. Bethany willed herself to move toward the light. Once there, she thought of Connor Jessup and a tiny spark shone even brighter. She reached out and touched the beam of light. Here was her destination.

A DEEP GROAN rose out of Connor Jessup's throat as he kicked back the bed cover. The action forced one of his boots to fly across the floor, but the sound was lost to his moaning. He turned over and punched his pillow, knocking a whiskey bottle to the floor. It rolled under the bed, leaving a trail of brown liquid in the dust.

"I don't need you, woman," he slurred in his sleep, his breath showing like fog in the cold room. His free arm hung over the side, searching for the bottle. Unable to reach it, Connor pushed himself halfway off the bed, looking under it.

There you are, my friend!

He grinned, grabbed the almost empty bottle, and downed the last few drops. He fell back against the pillow and groaned, flinging his arm over his eyes, his breathing began to slow and deepen once more and he welcomed the numbness. Whiskey-induced sleep had been his only escape from the memory of his wife, Elizabeth, leaving him for another man...

"Connor? Connor Jessup?" a soft voice said in the quiet room.

"Huh? What d'ya want?"

"I need to talk to you, Connor. I need your help."

"W-who said that?" He cracked his eyes open and saw a translucent being glowing like the full moon in the middle of his room.

"It's an angel!" His voice was a harsh whisper. He sat bolt upright. "An angel of the Lord come for me." Connor rubbed his eyes with the heels of his hands. "Didn't think I'd go this way..." He thrashed back and forth, groaning.

"Connor? My name is Bethany."

"I won't be any use to you in Heaven," he muttered.

Bethany shook her head. "That's not why I'm here." She took a step forward.

His eyes cracked open. He shook violently, his body covered with sweat. He grabbed the whiskey and started to take a drink, then tossed it aside. It bounced off the wall, crashing as it hit the floor. "Damn Clem sold me a bad bottle. That's what this is all about. Well, I'll have a thing or two to say to him!"

Connor forced himself out of bed and pulled on the lost boot, stumbling to the washstand as he did so. His hands broke through a thin layer of ice that had formed during the night, and he splashed cold water on his face. Grabbing the scrap of cloth beside the basin, he scrubbed it through his hair and face. Tossing the cloth aside he caught his image in the mirror and was shocked at what stared back at him—long unkempt black hair, torn shirt, eyes so bloodshot he could no longer see the brown of his irises,

"Need a shave," he mused, rubbing his fingers over the week-old stubble. He made his way to the heavy stone fireplace to heat some water but not before tripping over the cast iron kettle. Connor jumped up and down, holding his foot.

"I'll be damned," he cursed under his breath.

He limped to the hearth and tossed in some kindling. Striking a match, he fanned the flames with his hand until they were hot. He started to place a log on the fire, then froze.

There she was again! The angel!

From out of the waves of heat, a woman's form emerged. Again, she reached out to him. Connor threw the log at her. "Get away from here angel!" he shouted. Yanking his coat off the peg by the door, Connor pulled it on and stalked out of the cabin.

CHAPTER EIGHT

Connor trudged down the mountain intent on heading to town. Although it was only a short walk, the melting snow and slick mud made it difficult to keep his footing. Just when he thought he was in the clear, he tripped over the root of a tree and landed on his back. He got to his feet and slid back down again.

"Well, I'll be damned," he cursed again.

"And so you will be," came a voice from behind him.

Connor looked over his shoulder, spying a man wearing a fringed buckskin jacket and denim trousers. He blocked the sunlight as he came into focus. Connor smiled crookedly. "Jimmy Brown Eagle. How the hell are you?"

Jimmy smiled back. "Well, I'm definitely a might cleaner than you, that's for sure." He reached down, offering Connor a hand up.

"Much obliged," Connor said as he tried to wipe the mud from the seat of his pants. He finally quit trying, seeing that he was only spreading the muck around and making more of a mess.

"What you need is a woman to look out for you, friend."

"I had one of those once. Don't believe I'll be trying one again any time soon." Connor dug into the pocket of his deerskin coat and pulled out a small flask. He tilted back his head, took a long swallow, and then offered it to Jimmy.

Jimmy shook his head, the trade beads woven into his long braids clinked together. "No thanks, Connor. You know I don't drink." He eyed his companion as they began to walk toward town. "Neither should you."

"Don't even think about lecturing me today. I'm not in the mood," he grumbled.

"I can't stand to see you wasting your life this way." He shook his head. "For God's sake, Connor, you look like an old man. You're only thirty-six, the same age as me." Jimmy put his hand on Connor's shoulder. "Elizabeth is gone. She left a long time ago. You have to accept that and move on."

Connor shrugged off Jimmy's hand. "If you don't mind, I was headed to the saloon," he mumbled, making his way alone down the rutted street.

"Hey, Sheriff!" someone yelled. Connor stopped and turned around, scanning the battered wooden facades of the stores across the alley, looking for whoever was calling him. A young boy ran past.

"Sheriff!" the boy hollered again. Another man turned around, his silver badge glinting in the sunlight.

Connor shook his head.

Well, I'll be damned. Old habits sure die hard.

He pushed the swinging door and stepped into the saloon. He squinted as his eyes adjusted to the dimly lit interior. Spotting a seat at the bar, Connor strode toward it and sat down. He motioned for the bartender, a squat, stubby man named Clem Riley. Clem put down the glass he was drying and walked over to Connor. "No credit today, Jessup. You wanna drink, you gotta pay for it up front. Cash on the barrel."

"I want to know what you put in that whiskey you sold me last night. Were you trying to poison me? Is that it?"

Clem's eyes narrowed. "I ain't got the faintest idea what yer talking about." He turned his back to Connor. "Go home and sleep it off."

Connor's hand shot out and grabbed Clem by the neck ties of his apron. He pulled the man backward until he was against the mahogany bar. "I tell you that whiskey was bad. I been seeing things. It probably would've killed me if I'd finished the whole bottle. I want my money back." He shoved the bartender away from him.

"There's no money to be returned to you, Connor Jessup. You ain't paid for nothing since you got fired as sheriff. I only felt sorry for you, that's why I let you buy on credit."

"Take it back."

"Take what back? You don't have nothing worth taking. Since your wife left, that is," Clem snorted.

Connor slammed his fist onto the bar, rattling the glasses of a few early morning stragglers. The other men at the bar sat silently as they watched. "Take it back that you feel sorry for me. I won't have another man pitying me, Clem." His voice turned into almost a whisper. "Now."

Connor's right hand rested on the butt of his Colt forty-five. Clem shifted back and forth where he stood, a fine sweat breaking out on his upper lip.

"Look, Jessup, I ain't looking for no fight. Just go on home." He reached under the bar with a shaky hand. "Here. Here, take this." He handed him a half empty bottle of whiskey. "There's nothing wrong with this one. See? Someone already drank part of it."

Connor eyed the bottle warily. Then his hand shot out and he grabbed it by the neck. He tucked it under his arm and stood to leave. "You better pray this one doesn't have the same effect, Clem, or I'll come looking for you. Only next time, I won't be so pleasant." He scowled at the other men and trudged out of the bar.

Connor walked around the side of the saloon to the alley. He found an old wooden slat box, turned it over, and sat down. With his teeth, he pulled the cork out of the bottle, spitting it out. He raised the bottle and took a long draught. The drink burned his throat all the way down to his belly, but it was a good pain. A pain he enjoyed; the only feeling he had left.

He took another swig, then another until the contents were completely drained. Several people walked past, shaking their heads in disgust, people he had once called friends. Even Mr. and Mrs. McDougall, who'd treated him like a son when he first came to Devil's Gate. The town had hired him straight out of the army to be their new sheriff and the McDougall's had given him room and board until he got settled. A little boy waved and smiled. Connor waved back, but the boy's mother rushed him along.

"He's a drunk, Charlie," she said. "You must stay away from men like him."

"That's not a drunk. That's the Sheriff!" the boy insisted.

"Not anymore he's not." The woman turned up her nose as she went by. "Can't take care of himself, let alone all of this town."

Connor let the empty bottle fall from his hand. A drunk. The words twisted in his gut like a knife.

He eased his head back against the clapboard siding and closed his eyes.

Maybe I should've let that angel take me away…

"Connor, it's me again. Bethany."

He cracked one eye open.

The shimmering golden woman was back.

"What d'ya want with me, Angel?" he grumbled.

"I need your help."

"Why me?"

"Because it has to do with your wife, Elizabeth. Only you can help me."

At the mention of Elizabeth's name, Connor sat up.

A stray black dog trotted up to Angel cocked his head and gave a soft ruff. Smiling, she got down on her knees and rubbed him behind his ears. The dog panted and wagged his tail until a mouse scurrying past tempted him down the street.

Connor wiped the sweat from his forehead.

I guess I'm not the only one who can see her.

Wh-what did she say? Something about Elizabeth. He forced himself to his feet, trying to banish the image of his wife.

I gotta find Jimmy. He knows about visions.

Jimmy Brown Eagle was part Kiowa, and he was wise, and probably the only friend Connor had left. Connor stood and staggered his way to the smithy's shop where Jimmy worked.

CHAPTER NINE

"Jimmy? I need to talk to you." Connor took a step backward as his friend brought the heavy hammer down on a red-hot piece of iron. Sparks flew, singeing his coat. He brushed them off clumsily, but they had already done their damage. "Damn, Jimmy, watch what you're doing with that thing."

Jimmy glanced up at Connor and pushed the damp hair away from where it clung to his face. "Thought you wanted to be alone," he commented, tossing the iron into a bucket of cold water. He left it there until it stopped hissing, then pulled it back out again.

"Uh, no. What gave you that idea?"

"Probably your stomping off to the saloon by yourself. I believe you said something like 'I don't need anyone to lecture me.' Sound familiar?"

Connor shifted uncomfortably. "Hell, Jimmy, you know I don't mean it." He looked the other man in the eye. "Why, I actually like it when you tell me what to do."

"You're a fool." Jimmy snorted and tossed down the tongs he was holding. They hit the anvil with a heavy clang. "What the hell do you want?"

"Can we go somewhere private?" Connor asked, looking in the direction of David Wells, the shop owner. He was a big burly man with a penchant for minding other people's business.

"Sure. Hey, Dave, I'm going to take a break for a minute," Jimmy called over his shoulder.

David frowned. "Don't be too long. You got a lot to do today."

The two men left the building and walked along the sidewalk, the

53

old gray boards creaking under their weight. They paused. Connor leaned back against the wooden railing of the walk. He wiped at his mouth with the back of his hand.

"So, what's bothering you?" Jimmy asked.

"I'm not sure."

Jimmy sighed. "How much have you had to drink today?"

"Not nearly enough, I can tell you that. I still remember what she looks like."

"Elizabeth?"

"No, the angel."

"Angel? You saw an angel?"

"Yeah. Well, sort of. Last night, she came to me in a dream. I saw her again this morning in my cabin and I saw her a few minutes ago in the alley beside Clem's." Connor took a deep breath and looked at his friend. The other man was eyeing him curiously. "I know what you're thinking, but it wasn't the liquor. That's what I thought at first, too, but I don't think so anymore."

"No, Connor, I wasn't thinking that at all. In my father's culture, people are visited by spirits quite often."

"Well, that's why I wanted to talk to you. I figured you'd understand, being Kiowa, that is."

Jimmy laughed. "I'd think you'd want to talk to the preacher since it was an angel you saw and not a coyote."

Connor spit over the railing. "You know me better than that. Preacher is more interested in damning me to Hell than helping me."

"So, did this 'angel' speak to you?"

"As a matter of fact, she did. She said she wanted my help, that I was the only one who *could* help her. She also said something about Elizabeth, but I don't remember exactly what."

"Did this spirit have a name?"

He closed his eyes, recalling the golden beauty... "Bethany. That's it."

"Hmm. I never heard that name before. Maybe you should come to my house tonight. We'll have a ceremony to see if we can conjure her up again." Jimmy straightened and started to walk back to the smithy's. "What do you say?"

Connor didn't answer right away. He wasn't so sure he wanted to see her again, especially if she was an angel of death. "What if she's coming for my soul? What if it's time for me to die?"

"You worry a lot about death for someone who hates religion." He turned and looked Connor in the eye. "When you were Sheriff you faced death all the time?"

"That was different."

"Why?"

Connor scrubbed his fingers through his hair. "I don't know."

"I think you do know Connor. I think you lost something and you have to find it again. Besides, we all have to die sometime, some of us sooner than others. But when we do die, it is the perfect time for us. Do you understand?"

He nodded. "I think so."

"Good. I'll see you later tonight."

Connor raised his arm to wave good-bye. But his hand shook so bad he had to pull it back and hold it tightly against his side. "Damn," he muttered as he walked back toward his cabin.

"I DON'T KNOW if this is such a good idea, Jimmy." Connor's eyes were wide as he took in the scene before him. He had stripped down to his pants as directed and now stood still while his friend painted markings on his body. The heat of the fire caused him to sweat profusely and the paint began to run. "It's hot in here. Can't we open that tent flap?"

"No. We have to keep the steam in. That's why it's called a sweat lodge. You got to ease the poison out of your system. This'll do you good, considering how much whiskey you drink."

Jimmy sat and motioned for Connor to do likewise on the opposite side of the low fire. Next, he dipped a gourd of water and poured it on the hot rocks on either side of the flames. The steam quickly filled up the small wigwam, making their eyes water.

"Geez, you'd think you'd get enough of this at the smithy's."

Jimmy laughed. "It's not quite the same, friend. Now, if we're going to call upon this angel of yours, we need to be in the right frame of mind." He reached into a small suede pouch he wore around his waist and pulled out some dried plants.

"Got any whiskey in there?" Connor asked. "I sure could use a drink to steady my nerves.

"Your nerves will be fine in a few minutes. Here, take this." He handed one of the plants to Connor.

Connor raised it to his nose. "Doesn't smell too good. What is it?"

"Peyote."

"Peyote? You're not going to get me to eat it, are you?" He shook his head and handed it back to Jimmy.

Jimmy pressed the peyote back into Connor's hand. "Put it in your mouth and chew slowly. It tastes a little bitter, but it won't hurt you. The whiskey you drink is worse for you than these mescal buttons. Don't you want to find out what this spirit wants?"

Connor eyed his friend, weighing his options. On one hand, he wanted nothing to do with the drug. He'd heard stories about how some people went crazy after chewing the plant. But, on the other hand, he wanted to find out about the angel. He glanced at the button in his hand. He desperately wanted a drink... maybe the peyote wouldn't be too bad. He hesitantly placed it on his tongue and began to chew, his gaze on his friend. "You too, Jimmy. I'm not going without you."

Jimmy nodded, placing one of the buttons in his mouth.

"I don't feel so good," Connor said after a few moments. "I thought you said this would be all right." He leaned over, his head dizzy, his stomach churning.

"And it will be. The sickness doesn't last long."

Connor started to speak, then stopped. He straightened and held out his hands in front of him. For the first time since Elizabeth left, they didn't shake. Brilliant colors of red, blue, and yellow emanated from his hands. He waved his arms in the air, forming large swirls and rainbows. Jimmy splashed another gourd of water on the rocks. Out of the steam rose the figure of a woman, ethereal and wispy.

"What do you seek, Spirit Woman?" Jimmy asked.

"I seek Connor Jessup," she answered.

"Are you here for his soul?"

She laughed, the sound like small brass bells tinkling together. Connor leaned forward, bracing himself for the reply.

"I have no use for only his soul. I need his body, too."

"What do you want with me?" Connor asked. He reached toward the vision but his hand passed right through it, and she vanished before she answered. "Where'd she go?"

Jimmy shrugged. "She'll be back if it's important. Spirits never rest until they have done what they came to do."

"She said she wanted all of me. Am I to pass into eternal damnation body and soul?" He reached for the gourd. "Here, give me that. Let's see if she'll come back." Connor poured more water on the stones and, sure enough, the spirit named Bethany returned.

Bethany drifted from the fire toward Connor. He moved away from her. She stared at him and he noticed a blue glow coming from her eyes. He felt a slight pressure, right in the middle of his chest, as if her eyes were pushing at his heart. "What are you doing to me?" he whispered.

"Trying to help you, but I can't. You need to come to the portal."

"The portal?" Connor repeated.

"It's a place between the planes. It's where I am. It's where Elizabeth was. Come, Connor Jessup. You needn't worry." Bethany started to fade.

"Before you go, Spirit Woman, where is this 'portal' of which you speak?" Jimmy asked.

"Between the two straight rocks just outside Devil's Gate. Please hurry. I'll lead you the rest of the way."

Jimmy nodded. "We will come."

"Thank you," Bethany murmured as she left.

"What do you mean 'we will come'? Are you crazy? She wants to take me away."

"You have to follow the vision in order to understand it," Jimmy replied. "For now, rest. Sleep awhile. Before sun up, we'll travel to this place between the rocks to see what lies ahead for you."

Connor shook his head. "I don't know about all of this, but I have no choice. She'll keep plaguing me if I don't go. If I'm lucky, maybe the angel will tell me what she knows of Elizabeth before sending me to Hell."

CHAPTER TEN

A coyote howled in the distance, calling to the setting moon. Already, the orb was low in the west while a soft lavender and yellow glow rose in the east. Connor and Jimmy scrambled over the rocky, barren terrain that lay outside Devil's Gate. Every so often, a prairie dog would scurry past looking for breakfast. Connor laughed as one of the dogs stopped and stared, as if daring him to fight. He reached into his breast pocket and pulled out a flask. He took a long drink, then put it back.

"For God's sake, the sun's not even up yet," Jimmy commented.

"Doesn't count."

"What doesn't count?"

"I haven't been to bed. As far as I'm concerned, it's still night. I can drink all I want."

Jimmy shook his head. "Somehow your reasoning doesn't surprise me. You know, if you want to die so badly, why don't you just use that gun of yours? It'd be a helluva lot faster."

"I don't want to die, Jimmy." Connor stopped walking. He stared hard at the other man. "The whiskey helps to chase the nightmare of Elizabeth's leaving away. It makes living bearable."

Jimmy patted him on the shoulder. "I only wish there was another way."

Connor looked out in the distance. "I think those are the rocks the angel was talking about. What do you think?" About half a mile away, almost to the mountains, were two tall rock formations. The men started walking again.

"Those were the ones I was thinking of when she spoke last night," Jimmy answered. "I wonder if she's there."

"You know, part of me is afraid she will be, but I'm also afraid she won't. Does that make sense?"

"Yeah. In a way."

The men continued on through the desert in silence. When they reached the rocks, the sun was over the horizon and could be seen between the two stone towers. Its heat beat down on their faces, partially obscuring their vision.

Then, as if she stepped out of the sun itself, Bethany emerged, surrounded by a golden shimmer of light. It passed through her; the rays bending and casting streaks of color on the desert floor. She walked toward them. Connor and Jimmy took a step backward.

"I'm glad to see you. I wasn't sure you'd come," Bethany remarked, stopping about five feet away from the men.

"I want to know about Elizabeth before you take me away," Connor stated.

"I'm not here to take you away, Connor Jessup. It's your choice whether you come with me or not."

Connor eyed the woman. "It is?" He cleared his throat. "I mean, you are an angel, aren't you? Didn't you come to take me to Hell?"

BETHANY CONSIDERED HIM FOR A MOMENT. "Where is this 'Hell' of which you speak? I'm not familiar with this place. Is it another of the planes of existence?"

"Planes of what?"

Jimmy stepped forward. "Let me talk," he whispered to Connor. Turning to Bethany, he asked, "What is your mission, Spirit Woman?"

Bethany chuckled. *Spirit Woman.* She liked the moniker and decided to play along. "This Spirit Woman's mission is to request Connor Jessup's assistance in the search for my daughter. I believe he has information that will help me."

"Angels have daughters?" Connor asked, incredulous.

"I'm not an angel." Bethany glanced over her shoulder. The sun was rising and soon she would disappear in the light. She needed to return to Zachariah's before being trapped on Earth forever. "I don't have much time. Will you come to the portal with me? We can discuss my daughter and Elizabeth there."

She glimpsed the reluctance in Connor's eyes.

"Please, I must find my daughter. It's a matter of life and death."

Connor turned to Jimmy and the two men exchanged a look. Connor turned back to her and blew out a breath. "Show us the way," he said.

Bethany sighed with relief and passed through the natural entryway formed between the rocks and continued for several feet until she came face to face with a stone wall. She turned to the men. "This is it."

"This is what?" Connor asked. "It looks like solid rock to me."

Bethany sighed. "The portal. The place of entry between the planes."

"Tell me, Angel, what's this have to do with Elizabeth?"

"I don't have time to explain everything right now." She glanced up at the sun again. Looking down at her hand, she could see its definition was fading. "Please let it suffice for the moment to say she was a visitor to my world." Bethany touched the wall behind her and a slight crack appeared. "Will you come?"

"Why do I have to come with you? Why can't you talk to me right here?" Connor asked, his eyes narrowed.

Bethany took a deep breath. "Actually, I would prefer to talk to you here. The truth is, though, I'm out of time and can no longer stay on Earth. I have to return to my world. Now. Or be trapped here forever, as this shadow who stands before you."

As she spoke, the wall of stone began to shift until there was an opening just wide enough to pass through.

"And you say it's my choice, right?"

Bethany nodded.

Connor turned to Jimmy, gripping his upper arms. "Thank you for everything, Jimmy. You stood by me when no one else did and you helped get me back on my feet. I'll miss you, my friend. I don't know if I'll ever see you again."

"Eventually we all go to the same place, friend —the lodge of the Great Spirit. I'll be in the home of the eagles, just look for me." The two men embraced. "May you find peace and forgiveness, Connor Jessup."

Connor entered the opening behind Bethany, turning to wave as the rock closed around him.

CHAPTER ELEVEN

"Are we going to Hell or not?"

"I told you, I don't know about this Hell of yours." Bethany replied. "Perhaps when you're done on this plane you can travel there."

Connor shook his head and glanced around him, awestruck at the millions of criss-crossing lines of light around him.

"What is this place?"

"The light beams show all the planes of existence," she said. "You'll have to ask Zachariah if you want more details."

"Zachariah?"

"Please, Connor. Your questions will be addressed soon enough. In order to cross over to my plane, you have to close your eyes and concentrate. Allow yourself to relax and imagine a bridge stretching from here to that doorway over there." She pointed to a wall about one hundred feet away. A bright blue haze shone from its center.

"Why can't I just walk from here to there?" He indicated with his chin. This angel was becoming a real pain in the—

"Because of the planes of existence," she huffed, interrupting his thought. "You cannot move through them. You have to close your eyes and imagine a bridge and allow your mind to cross it. Then when you open your eyes you will be on the other side."

Connor looked ahead and saw a faint ripple of blue light in the blackness beyond the grid. "You mean there, where it looks like a waterfall?

"Yes, that's it exactly. Just concentrate and follow the path."

He pulled out another flask from his jacket pocket and took several sips.

Everything he'd experienced in the past twenty-four hours was crazier than anything he'd ever encountered in his entire life. Oddly though, he didn't feel threatened by Bethany. In fact, he trusted her. Something he hadn't felt since Elizabeth left.

Bethany frowned. "What does that drink do for you? Is your courage in that bottle, Connor Jessup?"

"You have terrible manners, for an angel." He scowled.

"I do not have the luxury for pretty manners." She crossed her arms over her chest. "My daughter's life is at stake."

Connor scrubbed his hands through his hair. "All right." He closed his eyes and imagined a bridge. Tentatively he took a few steps and was amazed at the solidity of it. The bridge that his mind had conjured actually held his body weight. Connor flexed his knees, bouncing slightly. The bridge swayed and he teetered, thrown off balance.

"Angel!" Connor yelled as he started to fall.

"Focus, Connor, and right yourself."

He took a deep breath and pictured a sturdy bridge with a handrail on either side. He reached out with his hands and steadied himself and concentrated as hard as he could until he reached the other side. The shimmering blue light looked like a waterfall from the other side of the grid, but up close it looked like a hazy translucent curtain. He wasn't sure where this would lead but he'd made it this far. "What do I do next?" he asked.

"Walk through the blue light and down the passageway to a door. I'll be waiting for you on the other side of the door." Bethany passed through the entry and disappeared.

Connor glanced over his shoulder at the pulsating lines of light behind him. They criss-crossed around him, bright and glowing. He took a long sip of his flask and slipped it into his boot then slipped his hand inside his jacket, feeling the reassuring shape of two more flasks in his inside pockets.

He stepped through the light and braced himself against the walls of the passageway as he walked, the whiskey beginning to take effect. He finally found the door and reached for the handle, his hand shaking. He walked in and to his surprise, found himself in an immense room full of stacks and stacks of books, the rows stretching as far as he could see. "I'll be damned," he murmured.

"Perhaps, but that's no concern of mine."

Connor swung around, startled. "Who the hell are you?" He raised an eyebrow at the frail old man standing before him. "You must be Zachariah?"

The old man nodded.

"You don't look like the devil to me."

"Well, I've been called quite a few names in my lifetime, but 'devil' was never one of them," Zachariah replied, with a quirk of his lips.

Connor noticed the man's milky eyes. "You're blind."

"My eyes are blind. But I can see you very clearly, young Connor."

He stared at the man for a moment, taking in the long silver mustache and purple robe. His eyes widened. "You must be Saint Peter." He slapped his hand on his thigh and grinned. "I'm not going to Hell after all. Damn. I thought I was in for an eternity of fire and brimstone."

"Yes, well, you still might be, depending on how well you do here."

Connor's smile froze. "You mean I'm not in the clear yet?"

"Mmm, maybe, maybe not." Zachariah shrugged, tapping his foot on the stone floor.

THE SOUND ECHOED throughout the room, reaching Bethany's ears. Her shadow absorbed the subtle vibration and gently floated along the silver tether until it rejoined her body. Bethany's eyes fluttered opened and she sat up and stretched. She rose from the chair and, feeling dizzy, grabbed the table for support. After a few moments, her dizziness abated, she was able to stand on her own. Her stomach growled and she remembered she hadn't eaten for two days.

"Zachariah? Where are you?" Bethany called down the aisle of records.

"Here," he replied, his voice muffled by the books.

She followed the sound of Zachariah's voice and heard another male voice rumble in reply to something the old man had said.

Connor is here!

It all came back to her — her memories of being a shadow and traveling to Devil's Gate to ask Connor to come with her so she could locate Connor's wife Elizabeth and find her daughter Sarah.

And what an experience that was. To be able to free-float, pass through solid objects, and invade the dreams of others. Never in her life had she been able to do that, not even while in the Knowing. It humbled her to realize how vast the soul's abilities were.

"There you are." She turned a corner and saw the two men. She bowed her head to Zachariah and then turned to Connor. "Welcome, Connor Jessup, my name is Bethany M'Doro."

Connor gaped at her. "It's the angel," he whispered. "But, how? I mean, I can't see through you anymore."

Bethany smiled. "Of course, you can't. I was in a shadow state when I visited you on the Earth plane. I've returned to flesh and blood now, the same as you. You are now on the plane of Keilah."

Connor's eyes shot back and forth between Zachariah and Bethany. He took a step backward and grabbed the door. It was no use. The handle had vanished.

Zachariah turned his head in Bethany's direction. "I was beginning to wonder if you'd return in time," he commented.

Bethany started to answer but was interrupted by Connor. "What do you mean?"

"Bethany had only two days to get whatever information from you she could. Judging from the fact you're here, though, I'd say she wasn't able to find out anything."

"You're right, Zachariah. Can we please go somewhere and talk? I've lost too much time as it is."

Zachariah nodded. "Come along, son," he bade. "Bethany can tell you her story while we have a bite to eat."

Bethany and Zachariah started walking. She glanced over her shoulder. Connor was following a few steps behind, his hand resting on a metal object tucked into a holder on his belt.

"They damn well better have whiskey here, that's all I have to say. To put me through this without a single shot surely would be hell."

CHAPTER TWELVE

"So, this is what it's like to be dead," Connor observed, settling into a heavy black chair near the fire. "If we're not in heaven or hell, are we in Purgatory?"

"You're not dead, nor is this place Purgatory. You're in the portal between the planes." Bethany explained. She had never met someone so caught up in the thought of being dead.

"But I am dying, though, aren't I?" He studied the back of his hand as he scraped his fingernails over the thick woven fabric of the chair arm. "So, this must be some sort of way station until I do and then you'll take me away?"

"We're all dying, Mr. Jessup." Zachariah sat down in the chair opposite Connor. "It's only a matter of time for any of us. You saw the sparks flashing on the lines when you entered the portal?"

Connor nodded.

"If you looked closely, you would have noticed the sparks jumped from one line to the next. That's death—a soul simply leaving one plane for another. Nothing more, nothing less."

Connor looked at Bethany, confused. "What do you say about all of this, Angel? Is this a dream or am I really here?"

"I say yes, you're really here and stop calling me Angel." Bethany was growing impatient with all this talk of dying. "I've told you, my name is Bethany and we need to get down to business. I have to find Sarah."

Before Connor could speak, Zachariah interrupted, "How about something to drink?"

Without waiting for a reply, he took the heavy glass decanter from where it was warming near the fire and poured a clear liquid into thin porcelain cups.

Zachariah offered one to Connor, who smiled his gratitude. Connor leaned over the cup and swished the drink around, taking a moment to smell it. Finally, he swallowed the contents in one gulp. He sputtered and began to choke.

"Personally, I prefer something a bit stronger than cherry water." With that, he reached into his inside jacket pocket and extracted a silver flask. He poured the amber drink into the cup and gulped it down.

Bethany and Zachariah shared a knowing glance. The man was obviously dependent on this beverage. Perhaps she was right when she asked him if his courage were in the bottle. Bethany thought about the ceremony Connor and Jimmy had made and remembered trying to heal the man. But, in her shadow state, she had been unable to touch him. She studied Connor more closely, deciding the time wasn't right to try again.

Connor broke into her thoughts. "That's much better. You want a swig?" he offered the flask to Zachariah who waved it away with a scowl. Connor shrugged. "Fine by me. So, Angel, as long as we're visiting and all, why don't you tell me about Elizabeth? You have to know that carrot you dangled is why I followed you here. Did you visit her like you did me?" He glanced away and stared at the flames in the massive stone hearth. "Or do you know her because she's dead?"

Bethany took a deep breath, trying to put her growing dislike for the man aside. He was weak, but he was also her only hope right now. "I'm what's called a Knower. That is, I can take an object and tell you about its owner."

Connor guffawed. "You're pulling my leg, aren't you?"

Anger shot through her, but she held her tongue. "Give me that metal object on your belt."

"My gun? No way. It's my only protection." He crossed his arms over his chest with an air of finality, leaning back in the chair.

"Then give me something else. It makes no difference what it is."

Connor stuffed his hand into his jacket pocket and pulled out a sheriff's badge. He tossed it to her. "Here, take this. I don't need it anymore."

Bethany placed the silver star onto the palm of her hand. She closed her eyes and, when she opened them, he gasped. "My eyes change to blue when I'm in the Knowing."

"That's a powerful trick you can do there."

"It's not a trick." She frowned. "Do you want to know what I see or not?"

He nodded and leaned forward.

"You made this yourself, out of a flattened Mexican peso. The coin was given to you by your father, a man who carried the news of religion across the prairie. You carved and carved on it with your knife until all the points were perfectly symmetrical. I see you squinting in the sunlight as you measure it. Then, you dug away at the coin until the word sheriff appeared."

Connor's eyes widened. Bethany continued, "You were a trusted man, you took care of Devil's Gate and protected the people. At least, until Elizabeth Jessup left you. From then, you began to drink heavily and were eventually replaced by another man as sheriff of your town. I can see you, sitting in front of a fireplace, consuming one bottle of liquor after another.

"The townspeople couldn't trust you anymore, Connor. They were afraid you wouldn't be there when they needed you."

She looked into his eyes. They were shining with unshed tears. "You have to make peace with this. Only then can you be free."

Connor wiped at his nose with the back of his jacket sleeve. "Yeah, well, I've heard that before. I don't need to be preached to by anyone, not even an angel. I made my bed and I'll lie in it, alone. That's the way I want it. And," he added, "leave my father out of this."

"If that's your wish." Bethany shrugged and tossed the badge back to him. "I work with a group of Diggers who excavate the area around Paran, the town I come from. During one of the digs, we found a silver box. I held the box and read it the same as I read your badge just now, and discovered it was brought to Keilah by your wife."

"How can you be sure it was my Elizabeth?"

Bethany's face softened, as did her voice. "I saw the scene when she left you. She must have been thinking of you when she came here because the memory was stored in the container. I watched her pick up her bag and walk out the door. 'Supper's on the fire,' I believe she said as she left."

Connor jumped up. "How can you know that? I never told anyone."

"You didn't need to. The Knowing told me. Please, sit down and I'll finish my explanation." She waited until Connor had eased himself back into his chair, then continued. "The box contains the Book of Eitel, an outline of the history and incantations of the Eitellans. They're an evil people, Connor. They steal children and extract their souls. The high priestess uses them to gain immortality."

"I don't see what this has to do with Elizabeth," he murmured.

"I'm not sure of the link myself. I only know what I saw—that you're her husband. I had hoped you would know what her connection to Eitel was. I saw a man named Michael Greene present her with the box containing the manuscript, but don't know anything else." She leaned forward. "Why was the book left on the Earth plane? How did she learn the writing? Did she talk to you about it?"

"Elizabeth was a headstrong, ambitious woman." Connor shook his head. "Michael Greene owned half the silver mines in Nevada and she was hankering after money. That's why she left me." He snorted and shook his head. "Sheriffs aren't rich. That's all I know." He looked up first at Zachariah and then at Bethany. "You didn't answer my earlier question. Tell me, is she dead?"

Bethany glanced down and studied the mosaic stone patterns in the floor. This was the part she had been dreading. She reached into her waist pouch and pulled out the ornate tortoise and mother of pearl comb. Her eyes caught Connor's and he slowly held his hand out for it. As she placed the object there, her fingers touched his. A spark of energy flew through her body, jarring her. She immediately withdrew her hand and looked away.

Bethany's eyes filled with tears as something inside her stirred. She tried to shrug it off. It was part of being a Knower, after all, to experience another person's pain and sorrow. "In my vision, Elizabeth and Michael arrived here in a bright flash of light. At the site, we found ashes and bone fragments. I tried to read them, but there wasn't enough substance remaining. I could only make out they were human and nothing more. I believe they were the remains of your wife and Michael Greene, with the exception of the comb and the box with the manuscript."

Bethany shook her head, reading Connor's unasked question. "I don't know how these two items escaped. She must have dropped them when the flames overtook her. I'm sorry, Connor."

Connor turned the comb over and over. "I gave her this on our wedding day." His voice was quiet. "It was my mother's." He leaned back into the chair. "I never wished Elizabeth any harm, I only wanted her to come home." Connor looked at Bethany. "How would she know to come here?"

"Legend tells us it's all explained in the Book of Eitel. It supposedly outlines how to travel between the planes without benefit of Zachariah's portal or death."

"I've heard that when you die, your life flashes before your eyes. That must be why you're telling me all of this — so I can remember the details of what brought me to this point," he said in a low voice, taking another drink of whiskey.

Bethany stood, wrapping her arms around her. It couldn't be. Her stomach clenched and she took a deep breath to quell the nausea that threatened. Here was her greatest hope for finding Sarah and it was nothing. *Nothing.* She walked over to the fire and stared at the flames, her back to Connor and Zachariah. The man knew less than she did about Elizabeth and Eitel. She lifted her hand to her mouth, stifling a sob.

Connor leaned toward Zachariah. "What's the matter with her?" he whispered.

"She had hoped you would be able to help her find her daughter. She thinks the Eitellans have taken the child and thought you'd know something, given your connections to Elizabeth."

"Me?" His laugh was bitter. Harsh. "Well, that's a new one. No one has wanted my help for a long time. Seems like most people I know can take care of things without me. Just like Elizabeth and Devil's Gate." He leaned back in his chair and exhaled loudly.

Bethany turned to Connor, her gaze blurred by her tears. She had expected too much from the man, she could see that now. "Well, Connor Jessup, if you're ready, I'll escort you back to the Earth plane."

"You mean I can go, just like that?" He looked over to Zachariah, who nodded. "Wait a minute. What about the comment you made about seeing how I did here? Did I do all right, then? I don't have to die yet?"

"You did what you could, given the circumstances and your degree of knowledge of the events presented to you. From here, Bethany will have to go on alone."

Connor studied Bethany. "Is there a chance Elizabeth is still alive?"

Bethany shrugged. "I would assume not, but I can't be absolutely certain at this point."

"Then I'm staying."

"You can't stay, Connor Jessup." Bethany took a step toward him, growing suspicious. "Why would you want to, anyway?"

He looked around him. "If there's a chance my wife is here, wherever here is, I want to find her." Connor stood and walked over to the window where the two suns rotated around each other.

Bethany turned to Zachariah. "I don't know about this. Won't he have to travel as a shadow, just like I did? What if we don't find Sarah in the two days given before he'd have to return?"

Zachariah tilted his head toward Connor. "He *is* emotionally involved, Bethany, like you—but there's a difference. The amount of drink he consumes clouds his thinking and his perspective. Given his altered state of mind, I don't believe there'll be any real danger in his getting locked into your plane. If he so chooses, I'll let him pass to Keilah bodily."

Connor turned away from the window when his eyes started to burn. "I don't know what you two are talking about, but this has been one hell of a day, I'll say that much," he muttered. "The way I see it is, I'm either dead—which you keep telling me I'm not—or I'm dreaming." Bethany started to speak, but he cut her off. "I know what you're going to say, but I'm not believing any of it. This place is too strange to be real." He glanced at Zachariah. "Especially him," he whispered.

"Thank you for the compliment, Mr. Jessup," Zachariah responded tersely.

Bethany giggled.

"There now, Angel, that wasn't so hard, was it?"

Bethany sniffed. "What wasn't?"

"To smile. My mama used to tell me a story. She said when it rained, it was the tears of angels crying over sinners." He walked toward her and his footsteps echoing in the great hall were the only sounds to be heard. "Well, this sinner has seen enough of tears. I'll help you find your child, Angel, if you'll help me find Elizabeth."

CHAPTER THIRTEEN

Bethany took Zachariah's hands into hers. "I'll return with Connor as soon as we find Sarah." She deposited a light kiss on his cheek. "Thank you for your help."

Zachariah chuckled, nodding in the direction Connor had walked a moment before. Connor stood apart from them, studying a painting that had been incised into the wall. "You'll have your hands full with that one."

"I know," Bethany whispered. "May the Mother of All grant me the strength to see this through."

"She already has, Bethany M'Doro." Zachariah smiled and took her by the arm, guiding her to the place where she had entered the portal. "Come along, now, Mr. Jessup," he called over his shoulder.

Connor took his time walking, all the while scrutinizing the sights around him—from the gemstone encrusted walls to the heavily patterned floors to the high pyramidal ceiling. To Bethany it seemed as though he wanted to imprint every detail into this memory.

"Are you ready?" she asked.

"As ready as I'll ever be." He took a deep breath as the walls of stone on the other side of the opal haze before them began to part. Bethany started to walk through, but he stopped her. "Wait a minute." Connor pulled the flask from his boot once again and drained the contents. He handed the empty silver container to Zachariah. "For you. It was made from Nevada silver by a friend of mine, Jimmy Brown Eagle."

"Perhaps you should keep it then," Zachariah said, turning the item over in his hand. The details of applied conchos and turquoise were beautiful.

"No, I want you to have it. You can add it to your art collection here. Jimmy'd be proud for you to have it to show."

Zachariah nodded. "Thank you, Connor Jessup."

"Don't mention it." Connor turned to Bethany. "Well, Angel, lead me to the Promised Land."

Bethany looked at him out of the corner of her eye. Promised Land? Would she ever be able to understand what he was talking about? She shook her head. "Follow me," she said, walking ahead of Connor through the passage to Keilah.

"WHOA-WHAT WAS THAT?" Connor froze just past the threshold, a deep vibration running through his body.

"It's from moving through the continuum, a reaction by the essences of your body," she said.

Connor looked at Bethany. The sun was behind her, casting a golden halo all around her entire being. He sucked in his breath.

Bethany pushed the long shimmery curls away from her eyes. "What's wrong?" she asked. "Are you all right?"

Connor's eyes locked with Bethany's. She was right about her "knowing" as she called it. When she looked into his eyes, it shook him to his core.

"I can heal you, Connor Jessup, if you'll let me," she whispered.

He studied the rocky countryside that lay before him. "You know, this place doesn't look a whole lot different than where I come from. The desert here runs straight up to the mountains and the land is as dry as any I've ever seen."

"Did you hear what I said?"

"Yeah, I heard you. My Daddy said he could heal, too." He started to walk. "Sorry, but I'm not buying much of it."

Bethany fell into step beside him. "What bitterness is this that you feel for your father? Can you explain it to me?"

Connor snorted. "Daddy was a tent preacher. We traveled from one side of the Mississippi to the other. His special talent was 'healing.' Mama and me, we'd sneak into the back of the tent and sit with the crowd. When he was ready to do his show, he'd ask if there were anyone who needed help. Well, Mama and me, we'd run up there as fast as we could."

"Were you and she sick?"

"No, no. You see, we'd just go on up there, before anyone else. Then, he'd make like he was curing us—calling on the power of the spirit and all. People would follow along, giving Daddy money to make them feel better."

"Are you saying your father was a healer or not?" Bethany asked, confused.

"Oh, I guess you could say he was. At least, that's what he told everybody who had a nickel to spend."

"I'm sorry, I still don't understand."

"No, I guess you wouldn't, being an angel and all. You probably can't imagine someone lying to folks. Telling them he'll cure their body and soul, then taking every last bit of money they had. He'd leave them with nothing, not even enough coin to feed themselves." He stopped walking and reached into his breast pocket. Connor opened the flask and tossed down half a swallow. He lifted it to his lips again before realizing the container was empty.

He flung it against a rock and the hollow sound echoed down the hill, mocking him. "Damn."

Bethany glanced at him. "How many of those containers do you have? Do you keep one in each pocket?"

"As a matter of fact, I do. The problem is that was the last one with anything left to drink in it." He shoved his hands into his pants pockets and stood still, again surveying the land. "I kind of figured Hell would be different. You know, the fire and brimstone?" He looked up at the sky. "It's too blue."

"What color should it be?" Bethany asked, her lips quirked in a smile.

"Well, if this were really Hell, I'd guess it'd be as black as the darkest starless night, with flashes of red fire against the horizon." He squinted his eyes as he looked off into the distance.

"What do you see?" Bethany asked.

Connor gazed at the stand of long needled conifers. "Just the ghost of a memory." Connor shook his head. "I buried my Daddy, almost twenty years ago, under some trees like those over there, right along side Mama. They both died of the fever, only a few days apart."

"How old were you?"

"Barely sixteen. I've been on my own ever since." He rubbed his eyes wearily. "Except for Elizabeth."

BETHANY STUDIED HIS PROFILE, trying to make some sense of the puzzle Connor Jessup represented. She could see the strength that had once been there translated into the way he held himself. And, more importantly to her, a strength of spirit that occasionally showed through the drunken demeanor. "In my world, a clump of trees of that sort would indicate the location of a kiyolo."

"Kiyolo? Is that anything like a saloon? I sure could use a drink."

"Hardly." Bethany picked up her pace. "Watch your step," she said. The ground was covered with sharp rocks, designed to deter intruders.

"A kiyolo is a place of prayer for the Eitellans," she explained as they hurried along. "Originally, these underground caves were used by an even earlier group of people, the Druas. When they disbanded, the followers of Eitel adopted the caves for their own use. At least, that's what the legends say. I'm praying I'll find some information here that'll help me find Sarah."

Bethany and Connor reached the brush around the kiyolo, finding it to be thick and heavy with the scent of pine. They pushed back the boughs and the sticky resin that coated the branches clung to their hands and clothes. In the middle of the trees, covering the opening, rested a large flat rock. Bethany bent over and struggled to move it out of the way.

"Let me help you," Connor offered. As he did so, he stumbled over an exposed tree root and fell forward, landing face first on top of the stone.

Connor grunted. "Got anything liquor-like around here?" he managed to ask between breaths. Bethany shook her head.

"Don't look at me like that," Connor whispered roughly, pushing himself to his knees.

"Like what?" Bethany struggled to guard her expression.

"Like you feel sorry for me. I won't have you feeling sorry for me."

Bethany reached out and pushed back a stray lock of midnight black hair that had fallen over his eyes. She gasped and pulled away, but not before she felt his imminent death. It was the same feeling she'd had when studying the Akashic Records and it welled up inside, overpowering her.

He froze, his eyes steady with Bethany's. "You're reading me, just like you did with my badge, aren't you? Tell me what you see, Angel," he whispered.

Bethany shook her head. "I can't."

"Please, Angel. Tell me."

She looked away. Why should she have such an intense sense of connection with this man? The only important fact about Connor Jessup was that he was going to help her find Sarah. Sarah. The thought of her daughter helped Bethany refocus and push aside the heavy sadness and sense of loss she felt for Connor.

"You know, I can't move this stone with you kneeling on it."

Connor glanced down, then scrambled to his feet. "Would you let me help you now?"

"I can take care of it. You just make sure there's no one around watching us."

Connor raised his hand to shade his eyes and scanned the area around them. "Nothing to report, Captain, Sir."

Bethany shot him a frown then returned her attention to the stone. She gave it one last pull and it finally slid along two tracks carved into the solid ground. Bethany stood and brushed the red dirt from her leggings. "I'm going in."

"Not so fast." Connor held up his hand and stepped in front of her.

"What do you mean?" Bethany placed her hands on her hips.

"It means I'll go in there first. A woman doesn't have any business running headlong into what could be trouble." He took a step down on the stone stairs that were carved into the side of the kiyolo.

"Hold on there one minute, Connor Jessup. I am perfectly capable of taking care of myself. I've been doing it all my life, even more so since my husband died. You have absolutely no idea what to expect when you enter that cave, whereas I do. I *will* go in there first."

"You had a husband?"

"Did you hear anything I said?" Bethany sighed, exasperated. This was as difficult as trying to explain her need for independence to Ian Johns. Didn't men understand? They themselves wanted it, but it wasn't considered acceptable for women. It was beyond belief that here was another man from a completely different plane reacting the same way. She shook her head. "Are all of you men alike?"

Connor puffed himself up. "Well, forgive me for not knowing angels have husbands." He looked away, shaking his head. "How the hell was I supposed to know? Then you go off getting mad at me, like I did something wrong."

Bethany poked a finger at his chest. "I will not stand here arguing with you anymore. My daughter's very existence is at stake and, while I appreciate your help, I want you *out of my way. Now!*" With each of the last words she spoke, Bethany poked him in the chest.

Just as she finished her tirade, Connor grabbed hold of her wrist. When he spoke, his tone was flat and low. "You talk to me like I don't have the sense God gave a jackass."

"Well, I won't disagree with you there. I don't know what a jackass is, but it sounds like a stubborn animal!" Bethany struggled to wrestle her arm free. She gave Connor a slight shove and, before either could react, he lost his balance and tumbled down the worn stone steps, pulling her with him.

The pair hit the bottom with a thud, stirring up a cloud of dust and sending what Bethany guessed to be several rodents scurrying. Slowly, she sat up, taking a mental inventory to make sure no bones were broken.

"Of all the stupidest things!" Connor rolled off his back and onto his side, trying to rub the pain in his right thigh away. "You're awfully damn clumsy for an angel."

Bethany whacked him in the shoulder with all her might. He yelped. She stood and looked down at him. "I'm *not* an angel."

CHAPTER FOURTEEN

Frustrated, Bethany left Connor where he lay on the compacted clay floor and began to search around the side of the stair. She ran her hands over the cool stone, feeling every bit of its surface.

"What're you doing that for?" Connor asked, now rubbing his shoulder. "I'm gonna have a hell of a bruise, thanks to you."

Bethany chose to ignore the last comment. "Every kiyolo I've been in has had a compartment where the makings of a torch are stored. It's just a matter of finding it." She glanced up at the opening they had just fallen through. The sky was growing dark and the first stars were beginning to shine. The crescent moon could almost be seen from the edge of the entry as it began its passage through the night. "There it is." Bethany spotted a niche set high into the wall. From it, she extracted a stick with an oiled cloth wrapped around one end. She reached into her waist pouch, searching. "Oh no."

"Now what?"

"I don't have anything to light the torch with."

Connor stood and dug into his pants pockets. He held out his hand to her. "Try this."

Bethany squinted to see in the fading light just exactly what he was holding. She wrinkled up her nose. "Why, it's only a rock. And a piece of metal. How in the world can that help?"

"Trust me," he said grinning, taking the torch from her hand.

"Not likely," she said under her breath, watching as he propped the stick against the stone wall.

Connor began to strike the two objects together, working to steady his hands long enough to make contact. Sparks flew until, at last, the torch started to smolder. He leaned over and blew at it until the fire started.

"How did you do that? You only have those two pieces. How can that make fire?" Bethany was beside herself with curiosity.

"Are you making fun of me?" Connor asked warily. He plopped himself down on the ground. "Everyone knows about flint."

"Perhaps they do in your world, Connor, but in mine, we use a liquid that ignites on contact. It runs underground in streams." Bethany picked up the torch and stuck it into a small round hole carved into the wall near the stair. "Of course, that can make for some terrible fires if you're not careful. Those stones of yours could be quite useful." She turned around to find Connor staring at her. Her breath caught. "Yes?"

"You say you're not an angel, but you move with the grace of one. The fire shines its light and you glow," he whispered.

She was both surprised and embarrassed at the tenderness of his words. "You truly have a poet's heart, Connor Jessup."

"Yeah, well, I used to like to read. You know, Shakespeare, Browning, all those writers."

"I'm afraid I'm not familiar with them."

"No, I suppose you wouldn't be. They're from my world." He gasped and doubled over, clutching his stomach.

Bethany rushed to his side. "Tell me where the pain is."

Connor shook his head, recovering. "I'm fine. Really." He forced himself to stand, still holding his midsection. "Isn't there some place around here where I can get a drink? It wouldn't have to be real strong, just something passable." He wiped at his mouth with the back of his hand. "I'm so dry I can't even work up a good spit."

"The best I can do is water," Bethany replied. "Based on the architecture of past kiyolos I've explored, there should be a spring in the altar room. Will that be all right?"

"I suppose it'd be better than nothing. I hope my stomach won't be too upset with me." He blew out a breath and straightened. "So, what d'ya say we have a look around then?"

Bethany nodded, her eyes still on Connor. "There's usually an antechamber just past this main entrance. Beyond there, we should find the altar room." She picked up the torch. "This way," she pointed with the flame toward the back of the kiyolo.

"Do you want me to go first?" Connor asked with a smirk.

She didn't reply, but gave him a narrow eyed glare. With a toss of her head, the long blonde mane shivered down Bethany's back. Connor hung back, watching the easy sway of her hips as she walked, a slight smile playing about his lips.

"Aren't you coming?" she asked, not even bothering to look back.

"Yeah, yeah. I'm on my way." He started to follow when a sharp pain shot through his body. Connor broke out in a cold sweat and leaned wearily against the wall of the passageway. "Wait a minute, Angel. I don't feel so good." He let his body slide down the stone until he was sitting on the ground. "Maybe you could bring the drink out here."

Bethany hurried to his side and crouched down near him. "Won't you let me heal you now? I tell you I can ease your suffering."

Connor studied her face in the torch light. He reached out his hand and, hesitantly, touched her cheek. "Can you keep me from dying?"

"No one can, Connor. If it's your time, there's nothing I can do about it. I can only make your remaining days more comfortable," she whispered.

"You said days. Is that all I have left?"

Bethany started to look away, but Connor put both hands on her face and forced her to look at him. Tears welled in her eyes as they changed from topaz to azure. "What are you doing?" he asked warily.

"Don't be afraid. I only want to help you."

Connor shoved Bethany away as another spasm passed through his stomach. "I tell you I don't want your help." He looked past her. "I don't deserve it."

"Everyone deserves to be well, Connor. The drink you consume has done this to you. Don't you see?" Her eyes shifted to their original color and she sat back on her heels. Shaking her head, she took the torch and entered the antechamber, leaving Connor alone with his pain and his demons.

CHAPTER FIFTEEN

"This is beautiful," Bethany breathed upon entering the antechamber. Here was a kiyolo that had yet to be explored by the Diggers of Paran, so it was still intact. The walls contained dark and colorful ground pigment paintings, each outlining a different event in the life of Eitel. Here, to the left, was his birth from inside of a kiyolo. *That's why the word translates into 'womb'*, she thought. She knew that some women entered those nearest their village when it came time to deliver. According to legend, it would ease their pain.

In the middle was a depiction of Eitel as a young boy. Surrounded by animals, his hands were raised to the heavens in solitary prayer. Bethany shook her head. How could one who seemed so innocent advocate the destruction of children?

Lastly, to the right, was Eitel as a man, fighting in the midst of a great war. Hovering over his shoulder was an ethereal being, painted in translucent hues. She appeared to be whispering into his ear as the soul of his enemy passed from the enemy's mouth into Eitel's. Blood and carnage were everywhere.

How did one person come by a power so strong that people would run to him, professing a belief in all he did? Bethany wondered. For surely, the man was evil and it was beyond her that his followers didn't understand this. But then perhaps they did, only they chose to simply accept it to further their own gains. *This new High Priestess is just another in a long line of those caught up in the greedy magic of Eitel.* Bethany shivered. When did legend become fact and why should her daughter be at the mercy of people such as this?

Bethany fell to her knees and raised her arms, tears stinging her eyes. "Mother of All, I pray that you keep my Sarah safe in your care until she's returned to me. Please, watch over all the children whose lives have been touched by this evil."

"Bethany?" a weak voice called from outside the antechamber.

"And help me to understand this man and my feelings for him," she muttered under her breath. She rose and made her way into the passage to find Connor standing again.

"Did you find anything?"

"Come. I'll show you." He took a few steps, then faltered. She wrapped his right arm over her shoulders and helped him into the next room.

Slowly, he looked from one wall to another, studying the paintings. "Whose life story is this?"

"Eitel. The founder of the Eitellans."

"Given his name, I could have guessed he was the founder. Thanks for the explanation anyway." Connor's eyes crinkled at the corners in a slight smile.

Bethany let go of his arm, letting it fall from her shoulders. "I'm glad to see you're feeling better."

"Mmm. So-so." He moved to lean against the wall, taking in a deep, ragged breath.

"Can you travel?" Bethany asked.

Connor glanced up, the sweat breaking out on his forehead as another spasm shook him. "Maybe," he managed to answer. He held his breath for a moment, then let it out slowly. "I could try."

Bethany fought against her instincts to run into the night, searching for Sarah. It was late and they could both use a night of rest before tomorrow's journey.

"That's all right, Connor. We'll stay here tonight and get an early start in the morning." She looked around at the images, feeling the eyes following her every move. "Maybe we should go into the altar room and sleep there. You wanted a drink anyway, didn't you?"

"Sure," Connor shivered and rubbed his hands up and down his arms. "Do you find it cold in here?"

"No, I'm comfortable. Are you sure you're going to be all right?"

He nodded. "So, where's the door to this altar room?"

"Over here." She ran her fingers along a line carved into the wall. "This is the entrance." Bethany shoved her body against the stone. It shifted slightly, creaking its protests at having been disturbed. She gave it another push and it opened fully, a fine stream of dirt falling to the ground. She thrust the torch into the room, illuminating the interior.

Again, the scurrying of small animals could be heard. Bethany shivered. "I hate rodents."

"Well, you're not alone. Sure you want to sleep in there?"

Bethany straightened her shoulders. "I'm not afraid."

"I didn't say you were."

"You implied it."

"Look, Angel, I really don't feel like arguing with you right now. Can we just go inside and get that water?"

"Of course, forgive me," Bethany answered, ashamed at having baited the man. Had she forgotten all of her duties as a healer? He was ailing, after all.

She waved the torch ahead of her and spotted another carved hole in the wall near the opening. Depositing the stick there, she went back to Connor and helped him into the chamber. They both stopped just past the doorway. In the center of the room sat a large statue of a woman. It was in a cross-legged position, its head almost touching the ceiling. The features were painted, similar to the murals of Eitel and it appeared that the room had been carved out around the figure. Bethany went to the statue and saw it was sitting on a flat stone base. Kneeling down, she could make out the cuneiform writing that covered it.

"What d'ya see?" Connor asked.

"There's writing here." Bethany started to decipher it when her thoughts were interrupted by the sound of trickling water. As lost as she was in this latest discovery, she'd forgotten to get Connor his drink.

Bethany pulled a small wooden cup from her pouch, turning it over in her hands. The geometric designs her father had painted on the outside were almost worn away. She was only a little bit older than Sarah when he made it for her. She approached the fountain. It was carved out of the side of the cave. The water ran over a large bowl and into a narrow trench that ran across the floor and under the statue, cutting the room in half. She filled the cup with the cool liquid for Connor and soaked her scarf for his brow.

She knelt by his side where he lay on the hard floor. Perspiration dripped from his forehead and ran down the side of his face, leaving streaks in the grime that covered it. Bethany helped him lift his head and drink. Slowly easing him back down, she wiped at his cheeks and brow.

"You have a gentle touch," he murmured. "You truly are an angel."

Bethany was glad for the semi-darkness as the heat of a blush warmed her face.

I'm twenty-eight years old, and the man's making me blush! Get a hold of yourself.

She could not allow her growing connection with Connor to interfere with her urgent need to find Sarah.

And what about Ian?

They were just friends. And Connor was here because of Sarah, and besides, he was ill from the drink. He'd been drinking so much that he'd poisoned his body and stubborn as he was, he wouldn't let her heal him. Maybe this was a sign from the Mother of All. She shook her head. She was being foolish. The man was dying and she seriously doubted his mental capacity. "I've truly gone mad this time," she muttered.

"Wha-what'd you say?"

"Nothing. I'm going to look around. You stay here." She folded her scarf and left it on his forehead.

"I don't think I could go anywhere, even if I wanted to." Connor reached for her hand. "Thank you."

Bethany's eyes caught his. She smiled. "You're welcome." She pushed herself to her feet, returning to the statue.

Running her fingers over the markings, she went into the Knowing. Before her, the visions of dozens of workers filled the room. Stripped to the waist, men and women alike, they toiled in the damp heat that prevailed in the cave, carving it from the surrounding rock. Their bodies glistening with sweat in the torchlight, Bethany watched as they carved the writing symbols into the stone of the statue. Small pieces of basalt flew through the air as they were chipped away.

"In whose image do you carve this statue?" she asked.

The memory of the scribe, still held deep in the stone, answered her question. "She is Yongi, the High Priestess of Eitel," the statue whispered its reply, its voice deep and reverberating around the room.

Bethany continued to stare in fascination at the vision. The workers motions were swift and fluid as they removed rocks and opened up the underground spring. The water flowed into the room with a great rush, spraying its coolness onto those standing nearby.

She should have guessed whom the image represented. The legends spoke of this woman, the first of the High Priestesses. Maud Hekate had told of her during the weaving of the story of Eitel. Bethany looked closer at the face and its solemn expression. Again, the scribe spoke, this time in response to her unasked question. "Yes, this is the same woman. It is she who is shown floating in the battle painting of Eitel. Yongi traveled from another plane, Junius, bringing with her the secrets to extending life. These secrets will be passed down from one High Priestess to another, as only she will be allowed to live on."

Letting the image of the worker fade away, Bethany ran her hand over a few lines of writing. 'Extending life' he had said. So, they weren't immortal after all. Depending on how many children they were able to capture, the Priestess's only lived on longer than their worshippers, so they appeared to last forever. That meant the Priestess could possibly be vanquished. But how?

Bethany released the Knowing and read on, thankful she had studied the ancient forms of writing for her job with the Diggers. The very last line told her what she needed to know.

"If you would seek my spiritual descendant's destruction for your own chance to ascend to power, you must not fear that which you would bring to her. The

laws governing the way of the High Priestess are revealed at the Kiyolo of the Night, one hundred sixty rods south, then due west following the path of the night star. But be warned. If you would waiver from your purpose, the price paid is forfeiture of your soul to the Priestess plus the years you have left to live as well."

CHAPTER SIXTEEN

The approaching winter blew its bone-chilling wind from the south. It swirled in the black sky and sliced through the clouds, caressing Bethany with its icy fingers as she climbed out of the kiyolo. She pulled her brightly colored shawl tightly around her shoulders, peering into the night.

I hope you're able to keep warm, my sweet Sarah.

Her heart clenched. If Sarah had been safe at home, Bethany would be telling her a story before bed right now. Sometimes Bethany shared sweet and poignant stories about her husband, Sarah's father. before he was killed. Bethany feared Sarah would forget the man who'd meant so much to them—she wanted her to remember him always. Other times, she spoke of the legends of their people.

The slight crescent moon had all but disappeared from sight, taking the stars with it. It seemed to Bethany they were trying to hide. Did the very elements sense the madness that radiated from her world? She took a deep breath, fighting the panic that threatened to take over, fearing she'd become immobilized by it and never find her child.

We'll be together soon, Daughter. I promise.

Bethany re-entered the kiyolo with an armload of dried branches. In the altar room, she found Connor dozing. In sleep, the stress lines on his face relaxed, making him appear much younger. As she watched, he began to stir fitfully, his body wracked with chills.

Carefully, Bethany arranged some heavy stones she had gathered earlier into a circle, then placed the branches within it. Using the torch Connor had lit, she started a fire.

Tomorrow's journey to the Kiyolo of the Night would be difficult. Though one hundred sixty rods wasn't a great distance to travel, the land formation to the south was treacherous to cross, especially with winter approaching. She would need her rest to face whatever lay ahead.

She curled up near the fire, laying her head down on her arm. She had to get there as soon as possible to learn how to defeat the Priestess.

I have to free Sarah.

"No! No!"

The screams tore through Bethany's sleep. She sat up in a panic and looked in the direction they had come from. There, to her left, Connor lay, his arms flailing about him.

"Get 'em off me! Get 'em off!"

She jumped to her feet. "What is it?" she asked, frantically searching his face and arms. "I don't see anything."

"Locust." He grabbed her shirt and yanked her down near his face. "You gotta get rid of 'em, Angel. They'll eat my eyes right outta the sockets!"

"But I don't see anything, Connor." Bethany pushed his arms out of his jacket and pulled it out from under him, hoping to find the cause of his distress. Nothing. She looked closer at Connor. His eyes were wide and glazed and he was sweating profusely.

Bethany closed her eyes and murmured a short prayer. When she opened them, she was in the Knowing. Quickly she scanned his entire body. "Oh no," she whispered. "What have you done to yourself, Connor Jessup?"

She focused on his aura, finding large gaps and tears in the various layers, most especially near his heart center. It was going to take a lot to cure this man, and part of her doubted if she even could.

She stretched her arms out straight over Connor and began moving them from head to toe. This motion would work the poison from his head, down through his body, and out the bottom of his feet. But just as Bethany was getting started, Connor again took hold of her. He wrapped his arms tightly around her, holding her hard against his chest.

"Elizabeth. I've missed you." He grabbed the back of Bethany's head and forced her mouth to his. Bethany shoved against him, punching and struggling to get away.

"Stop it, Connor!" she shouted. Finally, he broke the embrace, a deep shudder going through his body.

Bethany wiped her mouth roughly with the back of her hand. "Don't ever do that again!"

"Wh-what's the matter, Angel? Oh God, I'm so cold." Connor pulled his legs against his chest and wrapped his arms around them.

He's delirious.

Bethany fought to steady her nerves. This was going to be difficult. Once again, she went into the Knowing. "Connor? You've got to lay out flat on your back for me. Connor? Can you hear me?"

"I can't lay flat. If'n I stretch out the bugs'll come back. They can't find me if I'm all curled up tight like this." He looked into the darkness of the cave beyond the fire. "There they are, waiting," he whispered. Connor started to wave his arms again. "Go on home to the cornfields, locust. You won't feast on Connor Jessup today."

Bethany put a hand on each of Connor's upper arms and steadied him. She looked into his face, forcing him to turn over onto his back. "Connor. Look at me."

"No, no. You want to hurt me too." He thrashed from side to side. "Leave me alone!"

"I'm not going to hurt you. I want to help." She gripped his shoulders more forcefully. "Now, look at me," she demanded.

Slowly, Connor turned his eyes to meet hers. His dark brown gaze met her azure one and he began to calm down. "Breathe with me," Bethany instructed, taking one deep breath after another. He followed along and the muscles in his arms began to relax. "There now, that's much better." As Bethany kept his gaze steady, she placed her left hand on Connor's solar plexus. Slowly, she began to knead the area, working out the pain of his heart center.

When she was satisfied he'd calmed down, Bethany let her gaze once again scan his aura. Using both arms, she moved them over and over Connor as he lay still, his eyes closed. She started from his head and swept to his feet, leaving a long trail of bright green healing light. It settled like a fine smoke around him.

She took a deep breath and exhaled it out of her mouth. The breath glowed magenta, the color of the Great Mother, and swirled and circled Connor's body, working to close the gaps his aura had developed in this lifetime.

For almost two hours Bethany worked, patching his heartache and repairing the tears he had endured. Nearing the end of the healing, she placed her hands on his feet and kept them there until they were enveloped with a black mist for grounding. Continuing upward, she activated each and every energy point until Connor glowed with the renewed life force he now possessed from within. Yellow, orange, red, pink, green, blue, indigo, white—all the essences were in perfect balance.

Connor was finally sleeping peacefully, his breathing deep and even. She wiped the sweat from her face with a corner of her shawl. She hugged her arms around her waist, trying to keep from shaking. Bethany stood, then fell to her knees. She lowered her head and held it in her hands for a moment, until the wave of dizziness had passed. She tried to stand again but stumbled forward. Giving up, she crawled to the side of the fire opposite Connor. Watching the smoke rise to the ceiling of the altar room and drifting out through the entrance of the cave, Bethany fell into an exhausted sleep.

PART TWO

CHAPTER SEVENTEEN

Connor opened his eyes and stared at the rough-hewn stone ceiling of the cave. He blinked, bringing his sight into focus. Slowly, he raised himself on his elbows; something wasn't right. His arms didn't hurt. Connor sat upright and held his hands out in front of him. They didn't shake anymore. He stretched his upper body from the waist, savoring the feeling of being without pain. Lord, but he had forgotten how good it was not to suffer. For the last year or so, every bone and muscle had seemed to ache without end.

He'd assumed it was a sign he was dying, but now that it didn't hurt anymore, he wasn't so sure. Standing, Connor was surprised at how easily he moved. He spun around in a circle, his boots making a soft scraping noise against the dirt.

Connor clapped his hands together. What was this magical place that it could take away his pain? Elizabeth's face crossed through his mind's eye and he waited for the certain response he knew was coming–a sense of intense sadness followed by a need for whiskey. But, to his amazement, he didn't feel either one. And what was even more surprising was that he didn't care. He grinned.

I'll be damned.

Lord, thank you for liberating me from my pain.

He caught sight of Bethany where she lay near the smoldering fire. Curled up tight, she looked more like a girl than the angel he had taken her for.

He walked over to her and knelt down.

I'll be damned. My joints don't ache.

He shook his head. This truly was a miracle. Gently, Connor pushed back the long strands of golden hair covering Bethany's face.

He studied the spray of brown lashes that brushed her cheek and the small, slightly upturned nose. He sucked in his breath. He could clearly see her now for what she was and, though as beautiful as any angel he would have imagined, she wasn't a spirit, but flesh and blood. He reached out and caressed her cheek with his fingertips and, as he touched her, something stirred deep inside and Connor remembered.

"Thank you, Bethany," he murmured.

CHAPTER EIGHTEEN

The smell of roasting meat filled the kiyolo, invading Bethany's sleep. She opened her eyes and tried to ask Connor what he was cooking, but the words wouldn't come. Pushing herself up on one arm, she fell back down, still exhausted from last night's healing.

"I shot a rabbit," Connor explained from the other side of the fire where he was roasting the animal. "At least, that's what it looked like, except its ears were bobbed." He grinned. "It's hard telling just exactly what kind of critter I'm cookin', I just hope it's edible."

Bethany managed a weak smile. "Could I have a drink, please?" she asked, her voice raspy. Connor hurried to the fountain and returned with a cupful of the cool liquid. He supported her head as she took a sip. "Thank you."

"Are you going to be all right?" Connor's face was lined with concern. "Is there anything I can do?"

She shook her head, closing her eyes. "No, I'll be fine." This was the worst she had ever felt after a healing. Usually she might be a bit dizzy or nauseous. Then, she'd never dealt with someone as distressed as Connor Jessup. Although it warmed her spirit to know she'd succeeded, it had taken all of her strength to see him through the healing.

"I'll be fine," she said again with a smile and drifted off to sleep.

"Bethany?"

She opened her eyes.

"You've been asleep a few hours." Connor was crouched beside her. "I was getting worried."

"Mmm, I think I'm feeling better. Really," she added quickly when Connor shot her a skeptical look. "I always have a reaction when I do a healing. This one was just more intense than what I'm used to." She rubbed her eyes.

"I'm sorry I put you through this."

"It's all right, Connor. I had to help you. It's what I do." She smiled. "It's what I am." Pushing herself up, Bethany propped her back against the wall of the altar room. "How late is it?"

"Well, I was outside a few minutes ago and it's starting to get dark. The sun was about halfway down."

"It's sundown already?" She'd slept the entire day. Frustrated, Bethany let her head fall back and stared at the ceiling. "Why did you let me sleep so long? You know we needed to be going." She leveled her gaze on him.

"I understand you want to find your daughter as soon as possible, but you were in no condition to travel today." He took her hand and squeezed it gently. "I'm sorry for causing you this delay. It's all my fault. Please forgive me. If I do nothing else with my remaining time in this life, I'll seek redemption by helping you find Sarah."

"Thank you, Connor," she whispered, squeezing his hand in return. "We'll stay one more night, then be on our way at sunrise. We'll need daylight for the journey to the next kiyolo anyway."

"Are we going to another of these places?"

Bethany nodded. "When you were resting, I discovered that the answer to destroying the Priestess lies in another structure, the Kiyolo of the Night." She explained the information she had gleaned from the statue. "It's not far from here, but the terrain is difficult to cross."

"You lead the way and I'll be right behind you." He laughed, shaking his head.

"What's the matter?" Bethany asked.

"Don't get mad, but I'm not used to having a woman make all the decisions for me."

"I beg your pardon?" Bethany squared her shoulders, getting angry anyway.

Connor held up a hand. "Calm down, now. I don't want to get into an argument. I understand this is a different place and I just need to learn your ways."

Well, at least he was receptive to change, she'd give him that. Deciding to drop the matter for the time being, Bethany spied what remained of the bob-ear skewered on a stick across the fire. "Could I have some of that? I'm famished."

Connor laughed. "Well, then, you must be feeling better."

Bethany smiled her thanks as he handed her a slice of the juicy dark meat. Connor sat by her side as she ate. "Thank you for taking care of me," she said.

"I'm the one who should be thanking you. When you offered to heal me, I had no idea." He shook his head. "Absolutely no idea how it would be. Here, take a look." He held out his hands in front of him. "I can't believe they don't shake anymore. And I don't crave whiskey."

"I'm glad you're feeling better." Bethany took another bite of the tender meat and glanced at him out of the corner of her eye. He must have cleaned himself up while she was sleeping. It was the first time she'd seen him without a layer of grime on his person. "If nothing else, your looks have certainly improved since the healing," she teased.

"Yeah, well, when you drink the amount I did you don't worry about much else except where the next bottle's coming from." He ran a hand through his thick black hair and it shone a midnight blue in the firelight. "I found a stream near here and bathed. It was cold but it did the trick. I hope that was all right. I don't know the rules you play by in this world."

So, he had indeed accepted the fact he was on another plane and not in that *Hell* place of his he was so anxious to visit. "Are you disappointed, then, that you're not dead? You seemed so intent on it."

"Not in the least, Angel."

He leaned closer and Bethany caught her breath. Connor's spirit had returned—he now exuded a strength that had been buried under self-loathing and drink.

She let her gaze wander over his dark brown eyes, straight nose, and slightly parted lips. Again, she realized just how affected she was by his presence.

Why am I so attracted to this man?

She didn't know the answer to that. Where matters of the heart were concerned, she was better off trusting her instincts rather than searching for reasons.

Connor reached out and caressed her cheek with the back of his hand. "So soft," he murmured.

Bethany's eyes held his as he leaned even closer. She licked her lips without thinking and watched the reflection of the fire in his eyes. His lips touched hers and Bethany closed her eyes and let her head fall back as he traced a damp trail of kisses along her throat. Kisses as light as a butterfly's touch, stirred feelings she'd thought had departed forever after Joseph's death.

It's been so long…

Bethany slipped her hand behind Connor's head and brought his mouth to hers, hungrily meeting his need with her own.

Don't do this! He loves another. He's only being grateful for the healing. And you are far too vulnerable and exhausted because of what you did for him.

Bethany struggled to push the thoughts away. She was exhausted. The healing had taken its toll on her and cost her a day.

Remember your quest to find Sarah.

Tears sprang to her eyes. How could she even think of making love with Connor, knowing that her daughter was out there, somewhere, afraid and possibly hurt…

"We can't do this, Connor."

"Why not? I care for you, Angel." He held out his hand. "Let me show you."

Bethany shook her head, tears spilling down her cheeks. "What about Elizabeth? After all, she's the reason you agreed to come with me." Her eyes met his. "You still love her."

Connor frowned as he let his hand drop. "That was true before. But everything about her became clear when I woke up after the healing. I loved a memory, Angel, and mourned a future that might have been. That's all."

"Please, understand. I need to rest. I need your help to find Sarah."

He took Bethany in his arms and brushed the tears away. She lay with her head against his chest for a long time, listening to the steady beat of his heart.

"I understand, and it's all right. I promise, we'll find Sarah. I promise."

CHAPTER NINETEEN

The next morning ushered in the first of the winter ice storms to hit Paran, awakening both Bethany and Connor with the sounds of hail pounding against rock.

Bethany jumped up and rushed to the entrance of the cave, worried they would have to lose another day in their search. Peering outside, she saw the worst of it was almost over. Good. It wouldn't impede their progress to the Kiyolo of the Night.

"The sky's starting to clear," she called over her shoulder. "We're lucky we're not traveling any later in the year—the first storms are usually the shortest and mildest."

Connor walked up behind her as the sun came up over the horizon, breaking through the dark cloud cover. The light reflected on the ice shards and they glittered like prisms, each with its own rainbow of color. The ground was fast becoming saturated as the ice began to melt. "Your world is beautiful, Angel," he whispered in her ear. He pulled her back against his chest. "Just like you."

"Thank you," she murmured, enjoying the warmth of his embrace against the wind's chill. "We need to get going. I can't waste any more time." Bethany shook her head. "It's been so long since Sarah disappeared, I'm beginning to lose count of the days. It seems like forever to me. I've got to find her."

Connor turned Bethany around to face him. "We will, Bethany. I promise."

"And what about Elizabeth? Tell me, Connor, what are you going to do if we find her in the process?" Bethany asked, not sure she really wanted to know the answer.

"I'm not afraid of seeing her, *if* she's still alive. As a matter of fact, I look forward to the opportunity so I can tell her good-bye once and for all."

Bethany reached up on her tiptoes and placed a light kiss on his cheek. "Thank you."

"Whoa, what was that?" An eyebrow shot up. "I seem to remember sharing less chaste kisses last night."

"And you would discuss this in the light of day?" Bethany teased.

"I've spent far too long living in a gray cloud of my own dark thoughts. From now on, I'm going to speak my mind," Connor replied with a wink.

Bethany chuckled as she made her way back into the cave to retrieve her belongings. Connor followed closely behind.

Bethany wrapped her shawl tightly around her arms, knotting it in front.

"Don't you have anything heavier to wear?" he asked, scooping up his jacket.

"No." She shook her head. "When I left home, I wasn't planning on being gone so long. This is all I brought with me, but I'll be fine."

Connor walked over to her and untied the knot. "What do you think you're doing?" she asked. "You know we need to get out of here."

"And you need to keep warm." He slipped his coat over her and placed the shawl on top of it.

"I couldn't. You'll need it."

"My shirt is heavy, and I'm used to being out when the weather's bad." He grinned. "You think I had a nice cozy jacket every time I wandered off drunk?" He snorted. "I spent more nights on the cold hard ground than I can remember. So, this little ice storm and wintry wind should be easy to handle."

Bethany eyed him skeptically. "Well, all right. But promise me you'll say something if you need it back."

Connor made a cross on his chest with a forefinger. "Cross my heart."

"What was that you just did?"

"Made a promise. That's how we do it sometimes."

Bethany repeated the motion on her own chest, then looked up at Connor, smiling. "I like that."

"Well, feel free to use it anytime you need to," he offered with a grin. "Now, shall we go?"

Bethany nodded. "After you." She made a sweeping motion with her arm toward the entry.

Connor rubbed the heavy stubble covering his chin. "Wait a minute. First you want to be the adventurous one, now you want me to lead the way. I just don't know. Is there some danger out there I need to be warned about?"

"No, not particularly. I just figured you would appreciate taking the lead," she teased. "You don't have to, though, if you don't want to."

Connor chuckled. "I wouldn't be a man if I didn't prefer leading to following. Just nudge me in the right direction and I'll get us there."

BETHANY POINTED Connor to the south as they made their way through the thick tree line outside of the kiyolo. The sharp conifer needles dragged at their skin, the sap stinging the scratches. Connor took hold of a heavy branch, keeping it out of Bethany's way as she followed behind. Then, just as she was in its path, the smaller branch he was using for a handle snapped off, sending the larger one into Bethany's face. She screamed as it knocked her to the ground.

Connor rushed to her side, helping her up. "Are you all right?" She looked up at him, her left cheek covered with deep scratches. "Damn!" He pulled out his handkerchief and started wiping at the blood.

"My face feels like it's on fire. I've got to get the sap washed out of the cuts before they start to swell."

He reached into his pocket and pulled out a flask. Popping the cork, he poured the contents onto the handkerchief. "Your drink won't help, Connor," Bethany protested.

"It's water, from the kiyolo. I filled the flasks before we left," he said, holding the container up.

Bethany grimaced as he cleaned the sap out of the cuts. "That should just about do it," Connor examined the angry red welts on her delicate skin. "The swelling seems to be subsiding."

"Thank you," Bethany said softly.

He cleared his throat. "You're welcome."

Beyond the tops of the trees, a soft shaft of sunlight made its way to the forest floor. "It's almost midday," Bethany said. "We've lost a lot of time."

"We'll make it up." He scanned the horizon to the south. "It looks like we're almost to the edge of this forest. We should be fine after we get out of here."

"Don't count on it," Bethany stated flatly, starting to walk before Connor had a chance to ask what exactly she meant.

IT DIDN'T TAKE LONG for Connor to realize what Bethany was talking about. Just past the tree line, the ground was made up of large boulders of black obsidian. Its glassy surface—enhanced by the melting ice —reflected the sun, blinding them after the darkness of the forest.

Connor ran his hand through his hair. "Could be a bit difficult. Hey, look over there."

Bethany followed where he pointed and spied a break in the rocks. "Looks like a path."

"Uh-huh. That's what I was thinking. I was also thinking maybe it's just a little too easy. My guess is whoever is guarding the kiyolo created this path as a trap or a way to observe newcomers. Either way, I say it's too dangerous to take."

She nodded. "If the Kiyolo of the Night held the secrets of vanquishing the High Priestess, it would be to her advantage to have it heavily guarded."

"We'll need to find another way inside," Connor said, scanning the area. "Over there. It looks like a natural break in the stones. It'll be more difficult to cross but should be safer." He glanced down at the petite woman. "Are you feeling up to it?" He already knew what her answer would be, but he asked just the same.

Bethany arched a delicate blonde eyebrow and crossed her arms over her chest.

Her fierce expression made him grin. He wanted to wrap his arms around her and kiss her with all the passion in his entire being.

"There is nothing that will keep me from going into that cave," she said.

Connor nodded, his grin fading as he caught sight of a movement along the ridge.

"What's wrong?" Bethany asked. "Do you see something."

"I thought I did," he replied, his eyes fixed on ridge. "Let's keep moving. The sooner we reach the kiyolo, the sooner we can get out of here."

CHAPTER TWENTY

A guard dressed in a short black robe and leggings entered Liazar's private chambers. Immediately, the sentry fell to her knees at the feet of her mistress.

"There are two people, Ma'am. A man and a woman. They were last seen moving south through the obsidian fields. They're coming toward the Kiyolo of the Night, toward us."

Liazar stopped combing her long red hair. She placed the bone implement carefully on the table next to her as she considered the importance of what she had just heard. "Do you know who they are? Are they familiar to you in any way?"

The guard shook her head. "No, Ma'am. The man is tall, his hair dark, unlike anyone I've ever seen around Paran. His clothes are different, foreign."

"Foreign, you say? How so?"

"His shirt and pants are constructed of a heavy looking blue fabric. We weren't close enough to see much detail. It was the hair, though, that stood out the most. I've never seen anyone with such black hair."

"What about the woman? Did she appear different also?" Liazar asked, her curiosity aroused.

"No, the woman looks native to Paran. She had a slight build and long blonde hair. But she was wearing a strange coat. It appeared to be some sort of animal skin with fringe around here." She moved her hands across her chest.

"Black hair and heavy blue clothes, you say?" Liazar leaned back in her chair, stroking her chin. No, it couldn't be, she told herself. He wouldn't know how to cross.

"Go after them, Lettie. And whatever you do, make certain they don't reach the kiyolo."

Lettie nodded. "Yes, Ma'am. I'll send a group out right away. It shouldn't be difficult. After all, they only number two." She rose and started to leave.

"And don't kill them," Liazar called after her. "I want them brought to me unharmed, especially the man."

"HOLD UP, BETHANY," Connor whispered roughly. "I heard something."

Bethany froze where she stood. Surrounded by the sharp glass-like stones, she watched as reflections of her image bounced back at her. She scanned the area, but it was no use. The sides of the passage came up over her head, so she had to rely on Connor to direct her. "What is it?"

"I'm not sure. It's probably someone moving in for a closer look."

"What are you talking about? Are we being followed?" Bethany asked, her nerves on edge.

Connor nodded. "Ever since we entered this God-forsaken place."

"And you didn't tell me." It was more a statement than a question. "Why not, Connor Jessup? I have a right to know what's going on. After all, it's my daughter we're after."

"Look, there was no sense in getting you all upset and worried. It may have been for nothing. I'm used to tracking and being tracked. Besides, I've been keeping an eye out—" Connor stopped speaking and gestured to Bethany to look up.

"And a fine eye it was," Bethany commented. A woman dressed in a long, flowing robe stood just above, pointing a sword at them. She was flanked by several other figures dressed in a similar fashion and all armed in the same manner. "Who are you? What do you want with us?"

"Names do not matter where you are going." The woman turned to speak to the other women.

Bethany frowned. There was something familiar about her, but what?

One of the women spoke to the one holding the sword. "I don't know, Esther. The Priestess said we shouldn't harm them."

Bethany reeled. It was Esther, the one who had stolen her daughter. She looked closer at the woman and recalled the vision where Sarah left with the Eitellan. "You took my child," Bethany murmured.

"Quiet," Connor whispered roughly.

"What did she say?" Esther demanded of Connor.

"Nothing, Ma'am. She's a bit touched, if you know what I mean." Connor pointed at his head.

Esther nodded. "You two climb out of there, I have someone who wants to talk to you." She eyed Bethany then looked back at Connor. "It'll be your hide if she causes any trouble."

Connor climbed up the side of the black obsidian, sliding back down several times until, at last, he found a foothold. Once on top, he pulled Bethany to the surface where the other two Eitellans met them. "Well, this is quite a welcome," Connor observed with a smile.

Bethany elbowed him in the ribs. "What are you doing?" she whispered frantically in his ear.

Connor continued to smile at the women. "Just making friends."

"Enough talking. Walk ahead of us." Esther motioned with the tip of the broad sword.

It was obvious to Bethany this woman enjoyed being in charge. Well, if she got the chance, she'd take that sword from Esther and gut her with it.

As they picked their way slowly through the lava fields that were interspersed with the obsidian, Connor fell to his knees.

"Get up!" one of the guards demanded.

"I can't. Bethany, help me."

Bethany rushed to his side and kneeled down. Esther tried to push her away, but Bethany held firm. "I'm a healer. He needs me." As she spoke, her eyes shifted from topaz to azure. The guards took a step backward.

"Tell me, Connor. What's wrong?"

"Pull the gun out of my belt," he spoke quietly so only she could hear. "You know, the metal thing."

"I beg your pardon?"

"You heard me. I'm fine. Just do what I said. Pretend it's a healing tool."

Bethany nodded, remembering Connor had called it his protection. Well, perhaps it would help them now. She pulled the gun out and waved it around his head in a circle, then passed it over his chest. When she got to his stomach, she pretended to accidentally drop it. Connor scooped it up in a blink and jumped to his feet. Before anyone could react, he fired a shot at Esther. He caught her in the arm. She fell to the ground, dropping the sword.

Another of the Eitellans picked up the sword. Running forward, she screamed some unintelligible words as she lunged for him. One shot to the leg and she, too, crumpled. The remaining sentry stood still, eyeing Connor and Bethany. Slowly, she raised her weapon over her head. Before he could fire again, the woman turned and ran.

"Well, that was easy enough," Connor said, inserting more bullets into the barrel of his gun. He squatted and felt the two women's necks for a pulse. "They're alive."

"What is that weapon? We have nothing like it on Keilah. Can it kill?"

"It's called a Colt Forty-Five—one of the weapons of choice for law enforcement in the west." He looked at Bethany curiously. "Of course it can kill." Glancing down at the two women where they lay, he continued. "Any special reason you want to know?"

Bethany punched him in the arm. "Why didn't you finish her off, then?" She pointed at Esther. "That woman deserves to die!"

"Easy, Bethany. Maybe you should sit or something. You need to calm down."

Bethany took a deep breath, her healing nature warring with her need for revenge. "She stole Sarah from me," she gritted between her teeth.

"I'm sorry. But I can't kill her in cold blood. In any case, she isn't in any condition to bother anyone for a while." He peered at Bethany. "Are you all right, now?" Connor asked.

Bethany nodded.

"Good. You had me worried for a minute there." He scanned the direction where the remaining Eitellan guard had fled. "How many more do you think are out there?"

"I have no idea," Bethany replied, her hands on her hips. "The only thing I do know is that we're going to need help to get past their defenses. You were right about what you said earlier. It looks like this place is heavily guarded." She blinked hard and wiped her eyes, fighting the tears of frustration that threatened. "This isn't going to be easy."

"No it won't be, but we'll fight all the harder for your daughter. Where can we find help?"

"At my father's. He's there and so is Ian."

"Ian?"

"He's a long-time family friend."

"Friend, eh?" Connor eyed her. "How far is it to your father's?"

She studied the position of the sun and scanned the landscape in the distance. "Not far. I recognize the rock formations over there." Bethany pointed toward a rust-colored rock tower with small piles of boulders piled up on either side. "If the weather holds, we can make it there sometime tomorrow. I remember an abandoned Digger camp not too far from here. We can hide out there for the night."

"Sounds good by me. Now, let's get the hell out of here before they come back with reinforcements. He jumped down into the crevice and caught Bethany as she did likewise. Then he climbed up onto the other side and pulled Bethany up as well.

After Bethany and Connor had walked for several rods, the obsidian gave way to small brown and black stones. Beyond that was another tree line, but there were no conifers this time, only broadleafs. The leaves were few as the winter frosts had damaged and killed most of them.

"These'll be much easier to pass through," Bethany remarked. "They don't have that evil stinging sap the conifers possess. The camp is somewhere near here. On the other side of these trees, I think."

Passing through the woods, they spied the small, makeshift village. "You were right, Bethany. Looks like an old mining ghost town, with those small clapboard houses," Connor commented.

"We *are* miners, of sorts, except we don't dig for treasures, we dig for the past."

Approaching the cabins, Bethany and Connor walked from building to building, looking for the least damaged one in which to spend the night. There had been no digging in this area for years and the cabins were badly neglected. Bethany shook her head. Who would have guessed the Kiyolo of the Night lay just on the other side of the woods?

Finally, they found a cabin with the roof and sides still intact. Bethany pulled the door open.

"Home sweet home," Connor said upon entering the old dwelling. The inside walls were weathered silvery-gray wood. He took a step forward and the floorboards creaked under his weight. He held out his arm, stopping Bethany.

"What's the matter?" she asked.

"Wait a minute while I test this floor. They feel rotten."

Bethany pushed past him. "Don't be ridiculous, Connor. This place was constructed of truewood. It never rots. How do you think these cabins have survived for so long?" She opened the only window in the one room shanty. It was musty, but at least it would provide protection from any ice storms they may get later that evening.

"Wood that doesn't rot? I've never heard of such a thing. What do you do when you want to get rid of it?"

"Burn it." Bethany smiled. "Now why don't you see if you can find some wood for a fire? If you want, you could probably use some from the cabin next door. It looks like it's beyond repair anyway." Bethany began to shake out the blankets that had been left piled in the corner, stirring up a great cloud of dust.

Connor started coughing, waving his arm in front of him. "I'd be happy too, if only to get out of this infernal twister you're creating."

She stopped shaking the coverlet. "All right. I'm done. Now, off with you. I'm worried about being able to keep warm tonight. We might have a roof and four walls, but their ability to insulate against the cold is questionable at best."

"You know, we might just have to rely on body heat to keep us cozy. I've had to do that before, when I was stranded out in the desert at night."

"And who did you keep cozy with?" Bethany asked with a raised eyebrow.

"Uh, no one you'd know."

"That's a safe bet I'd say." Bethany walked over to the fireplace, shaking her head. Picking up a small broom fashioned from twigs, she began to brush out the remains of the last fire that had been lit here.

Connor approached her, putting his hand on her shoulder. "Angel," he began.

Bethany's breath caught in her throat. She wanted to lean into Connor. Wanted his arms around her but not now, not like this. Not when she was so worried about Sarah and he was just waking up from his drunken grief about Elizabeth. "Whatever conversation we need to have will have to wait until after we get Sarah back home," she said softly. "Please."

His deep sigh tickled the fine hairs on the back of her neck. "All right," he said. "I'll be back later."

She glanced over her shoulder and watched Connor as he strode out the door. She smiled in spite of herself. Remembering his embrace of the night before, she hugged her arms tightly about her. There was something familiar and comforting about his touch. If they had to share bodily warmth, could they keep from becoming intimate?

CHAPTER TWENTY-ONE

The night ushered in another ice storm and the shards beat incessantly at the roof of the small wood dwelling. Bethany stood with one hand resting on the primitive shelf the previous owner had placed over the fireplace. Glancing up, she worried the flat shingles wouldn't hold together. It wasn't unusual for the sharp hail to break through a thin piece of wood or tear into a person's skin if it hit at the right angle. At least if it did break through, the impact would be softened and the ice could do no further damage to either of them.

Connor squatted and added another log to the fire. "It sounds like a rock slide out there," he said in a loud voice so he could be heard over the din.

"This storm is mild compared to some we've had," Bethany said, tying her shawl snuggly around her waist. "You should be here when we have a real one."

"I hope I am." Connor's gaze was warm with the fire's glow.

Bethany gave him a shaky smile. The prospect of spending the night with him in such close quarters left her trembling from head to toe. "I'm going to see how it looks outside." She walked over to the door and pushed it open slightly. The sky was a deep green, the horizon tinged with purple and she could see no end to the storm. Bethany pulled the door closed with a sigh, standing with her back against it. It looked like they would be there for a while, maybe even longer than just one night. *Will I ever find my child?* she wondered as a chill went through her body.

"How's it look out there?"

"Not good. I don't know if we'll be able to travel tomorrow—" she whispered in a broken voice. She took a deep breath. She ached with the need to hold her baby girl.

I need to be strong. I will see Sarah again.

She glanced at Connor. He sat with his profile to her, studying the flames as they shot out of the old shale hearth, dancing with a life of their own. Could she believe him where Elizabeth was concerned?

Bethany turned to the wooden counter next to the door, careful not to lean against it, for any pressure would surely send it crashing to the floor. Slowly, she began to assemble the food they had gathered after arriving, before the storm hit. She needed something to do that would force the haunting thoughts away from her mind.

Pulling a simple tin tray down from the shelf over the work area, she smiled, thinking of Connor's reaction to the different creatures living in the woods around the camp. One animal in particular, the doha, had caught his attention. Typically a domesticated creature, this one had apparently gone wild and wanted nothing to do with either of them. He kept comparing it to something called a 'horse'. Horse. What a silly name. She couldn't help but smile.

"What's so amusing?" Connor asked, walking over to the small rickety table where Bethany had placed the tray of food.

"Oh, nothing. I was just thinking of you trying to ride the doha this afternoon. How *is* your backside?"

Connor puffed himself up. "It's just fine, thank you. By the way, why'd you lead me to believe the damn thing wouldn't mind being ridden?"

Bethany shrugged, her expression innocent. "Well, they usually let you. I guess this one just wasn't feeling too accommodating."

He came to her, smiling in spite of himself. "Why don't we sit by the fire while we eat. I've already spread out a few of the blankets," Connor said. "You look like you need to warm up."

Before she could answer, Connor took the tray from her and placed it on the floor in front of the fireplace and sat on the blanket. "So, tell me what this food is."

Bethany sat down cross-legged next to the tray. "Well, the green leaves are called mellet. You take one and put some of these brown seeds—they're called plankas—on top of the leaf and roll it up. Then you eat it," she explained, popping one into her mouth.

Connor did likewise. "Not bad. Tastes a little nutty, like fried corn," he commented. "What are those?"

"Hmm. I'm afraid to tell you."

"Why?" he asked, his eyes narrowing. "Do they have a strange name? Or just a bad taste?"

"No, they're actually quite good." She held one of the large juicy red berries out to him, between her thumb and forefinger. "Here, try one. They ripen with the first frost."

He hesitated for a moment then leaned in, taking it from her with his mouth, his lips touching her fingers as he did so. "You're right. It does taste good." He winked at her.

"And you're incorrigible." Bethany smiled, leaning back on one elbow. She stretched her legs out, kicking off her kidskin boots in the process and warmed her bare feet near the fire. Her long hair fell over her shoulders in a soft golden cloud.

"You didn't tell me the name yet," Connor said, popping another sweet berry into his mouth.

Bethany stared into the fire as she spoke. "They're called Paran's Love."

"Isn't that the name of your town's founder?"

"Yes. It was named for him. You see, according to legend, when Paran lost his wife, he cried without end for three days. On the fourth day, a bush sprang forth from the ground that had been soaked with his tears. On it grew these berries, full of the sweetness of his love for her." She rolled onto her stomach, her eyes catching Connor's. "The Mother of All was so moved by the intensity of his emotion, She returned his wife to him, saying She had never seen such depth of love and it wasn't right that they should be parted. It's traditional for a husband to share these berries with his wife on the anniversary of their marriage."

"Did your husband share these with you?"

Bethany nodded. "As I said, it's a tradition. A way of renewing your feelings and commitment to each other."

"You must miss him a great deal." He reached out and pushed her hair away from her eyes. "Did someone heal you when he died?"

"Grief is a part of life, Connor. I would not be cured of it. It's made me stronger and more appreciative of what I *do* have," she explained quietly. "Joseph was a good man and I loved him deeply. At the time of his death, I never thought I'd be able to love anyone like that again. I didn't want to."

"And what about now, Angel?" Connor asked, his voice moving through her like a warm wave.

"I do." Bethany watched as Connor's eyes grew even darker and she realized that it was these eyes that held her captive. His gaze touched her, made her feel as if she'd known him across lifetimes.

Perhaps Zachariah was right. Maybe the Mother of All has blessed me.

Not knowing what lay ahead and needing someone other than herself for strength, Bethany pushed aside her worries and fears about the future. "Listen…The storm is over," she whispered.

Connor touched her lips with his fingertips. "No, it's just beginning."

CHAPTER TWENTY-TWO

Connor picked up a Paran's Love and offered it to Bethany. "Will you accept this from me?" he asked softly, his voice expectant.

Bethany considered him for a moment as her heart spoke to her, then smiled. She held out her hand to take it from him.

He shook his head. "Uh-uh. Open your mouth."

She complied and he placed the berry on her tongue, his fingers lingering. She bit into it and the delicious warm juice ran down the sides of her mouth. She giggled, wiping at it with the back of her hand.

Connor moved closer to Bethany, his eyes focused on hers. Moving closer still, he caught her mouth in a deep kiss. Gently, he urged her lips apart, probing until their tongues touched.

Bethany sighed and the kiss deepened, his scent filling her senses. Connor wrapped his arms around her and she reveled in the strength of his embrace. Rolling her onto her back, he licked at her chin until the juice was gone. Then, their mouths locked together in another kiss.

Bethany reached up and began to unbutton his shirt. She pushed it off his shoulders and ran her hands over the thick fur of his chest, feeling his muscles contract as he raised himself, kneeling above her.

Connor removed his shirt and tossed it aside. He reached down and unfastened the ties of her long blouse. Bethany shivered.

"Are you cold? I can put more wood on the fire," Connor offered, his voice thick and low.

Bethany shook her head. "It's not the cold that's making me shiver." She smiled, nudged him onto his back and straddled him.

Connor arched a thick dark brow, and chuckled. "Another one of your ways I should get used to?"

She nodded and giggled. Moving her shoulders in a circular

motion, Bethany let her blouse slide off her shoulders. Connor's gasp filled her with pleasure. She grazed her breasts against his chest, enjoying the rough texture of his wiry hair against her soft skin. "Perhaps you're used to taking virgins," she teased. "They usually lie back without knowing what to do." She pushed herself up lazily and stood, untying her leggings. "Of course, if you think I might be too much for you, we can stop now."

Bethany let the loose pants drop to the floor and kicked them away. Connor sucked in his breath. Bethany knew she had him. He held out his hand to her. "There'll be no stopping tonight, Angel. Come to me and take what you will. I'll give it gladly and take what you offer in return."

Clasping his hand, Bethany allowed herself to be pulled down on top of him. She smiled seductively and started to remove his pants.

"Let me." With a swift motion, he unbuttoned the heavy denim trousers and removed them. She lowered herself back down, squeezing his trim hips tightly with her thighs.

"You're so beautiful, Angel," he whispered against her neck.

His mouth found a tender spot behind her ear and sucked at it gently, sending shivers of delight through her body. "Mmm, that feels nice," she purred, her voice low and hushed. She tilted her head to the side, baring more of her neck, and her hair fell about them like a golden blanket.

Connor moved his lips along her collarbone, leaving a wet line of kisses. "I love the taste of you," he murmured.

Bethany gazed into his eyes and saw a hunger there that matched her own. He ran his hands down her back, lightly strumming her spine. His hands came to rest on her hips, urging her to move up slightly. As she shifted, Bethany's mouth came down hard on his in a demanding kiss. "You feel wonderful against me," she whispered.

"Angel." Connor rasped, as they kissed again, letting his hands explore every soft, warm part of her. He ran his fingertips along her sides in one long caress, then over her chest, stopping to massage the small round breasts. Raising his head slightly, Connor took one nipple and then the other into his mouth, slowly running his tongue over the tips, teasing them into hardness.

Bethany looked down at him, her eyes wide. "What are you doing?"

"Do you want me to stop?" He lay poised, ready to take the peak again.

She shook her head and lowered herself slightly until his mouth was on her breast. "We don't do this here," she whispered as he suckled. "Only babies."

"Our babies, too." He nuzzled his face between the smooth yielding mounds. "And during lovemaking." Connor moved his mouth downward, forcing her to shift with the pressure of his kisses. He gently pushed her shoulders until she was sitting up, straddling his chest. Connor ran his hands down her back and cupped her buttocks. With a gentle pressure, he urged her forward still.

Her eyes caught his and darkened. Slowly, she moved until her thighs rested on either side of his face, his whiskers rubbing against the delicate skin.

Tenderly, Connor spread open the soft, damp flesh with his fingers. He closed his eyes and ran his tongue over her in one long caress. Bethany gasped and arched toward him as he found her sensitive core.

Connor continued to tease and lick, relishing Bethany's moans of pleasure. She clutched his head, holding him tightly between her legs. He answered Bethany's need by probing her deep sweetness with his tongue, darting in and out faster and faster until the spasms of her release throbbed against his tongue. She called out his name over and over, as though it were a mantra as he continued to massage her through her release.

"That was heavenly," she sighed. Bethany raised her arms and lifted her hair, letting it fall a little at a time as she stretched. Slowly, she let her body glide downward, dragging herself against him until her mouth found his. "I want you now," she whispered.

"Take me then," Connor moaned. His strong hands massaged her buttocks, guiding her to his hardness. Bethany lowered herself onto him and began to move her hips, undulating against him. The wetness he had created with his kisses surrounded his erection and welcomed him wholly. Moving slowly at first, Bethany increased her tempo, caressing him from within using short, tight squeezes.

"My God," he breathed, his words catching in his throat.

He fought to hold on, to make her pleasure last longer, but when she leaned close to his ear and whispered her encouragement, he was lost.

"Let go, Connor. Love me...Love me."

"I will love you, Angel." He grasped her waist and moved faster, driving her up and down with the force of his hips. She braced her hands against his chest and matched his rhythm.

She placed her fingertips against Connor's lips. "Make them wet for me," she bade. He began to suck her fingers, licking and nibbling them. Pulling her hand away, she placed it between her legs, massaging the soft tender mound of flesh. She threw her head back and screamed his name as her muscles tightened and contracted around Connor. "Now, Connor," she gasped. "I want to feel your release, deep inside me."

Connor continued to move with full penetrating strokes, his hard shaft thrusting in and out until she sang out his name once more. Another deep stroke and his own shouts of ecstasy joined hers.

Moments later, he opened his eyes and his breath caught—he was in complete and utter awe of Bethany's glowing beauty.

He wrapped his hands in her hair, pulling her to him for a tender kiss, no words were spoken.

No words were needed.

CHAPTER TWENTY-THREE

Bethany awoke just before dawn. She lay still, her head in the crook of Connor's arm, savoring the warmth and closeness of his strength. Through a crack in the side of the cabin wall, she watched the sun begin its ascent in the gray sky. The fallen ice shards that clung to the trees outside glittered in the early morning light.

She murmured her morning prayers, asking the Mother of All for aid and protection for what lay ahead.

Connor stirred, and she lifted herself on one elbow. "Peace to you, Connor Jessup," she bade him, brushing a wisp of black hair out of his eyes.

"Good morning, Angel."

"Why do you call me that? You *have* to know I'm not an angel by now."

Connor grinned. "But I like 'Angel'. It's what I thought you were when I first met you. It's how I'll always think of you."

"Mmm…" She glanced at him out of the corner of her eye. "I don't have a choice, do I?"

"Absolutely none." He pulled Bethany to him, his mouth touching hers in a light kiss. "Are we heading to your home today or do I have to stay cooped up with you here?" He rolled his eyes in an exaggerated show of mock dismay.

"No, I think you'll be safe from me today. I was watching the sky before you woke up." She pointed toward the slight opening in the wall. "As long as it's not storming, we should be fine."

Connor stood and pulled Bethany to her feet. The blankets fell away as he did so. He scooped one up and wrapped it around her shoulders, pulling it together in the front and sighed.

"What is it?" Bethany asked.

"You're so beautiful." He pulled her close, wrapping his arms around her. "I find such peace in your presence, Bethany. A peace I never knew was possible. I want you to feel this, too." He held her at arm's length, his strong hands cupping her cheeks.

Tears welled in her eyes. "My daughter is my peace, Connor. Until I know what's become of her, there will be none for me."

Connor pulled her close again. "We'll find her. If not today, then the next. This is my promise to you."

As BETHANY GATHERED up the remaining food, Connor brought water into the cabin with a wooden bucket he'd found under the counter. He washed quickly, for the water was cold. Then dressed and fetched more water for Bethany.

Pulling on his boots, he watched Bethany intently, noticing fresh tears. "Are you going to be all right?" he asked.

Bethany didn't answer right away. She took a deep breath. Picking up the shawl full of food, she tied a knot in the material and secured it to her belt.

"Bethany?"

Bethany's eyes met his, her bottom lip quivering. "It's all right." She folded a blanket over her arm and handed it to Connor. "Here. This should help you keep warm until we reach Papa's house."

Connor rubbed his chin thoughtfully. If someone questioned his appearance word might get back to the High Priestess of their location and who knows what would happen then. They needed the element of surprise when they returned to the Kiyolo of the Night. "Do the people of your town look and dress like you? Are they fair-haired?"

Bethany looked down at her clothes. "Yes, for the most part. Except, of course, for this big coat of yours. Our coloring runs from light blonde to dark red. Why do you ask?"

"I imagine I'll look a might out of place, then, don't you think?"

Her eyes widened. "I hadn't considered the possibility of someone questioning your appearance. Bethany took the blanket from him and draped it over his head and shoulders, covering his dark hair. "How about this?"

"Fine, but what about my beard? I could definitely use a shave."

Bethany turned to the shelf over the old counter. Taking down a small wooden box, Bethany handed it to him. "Here."

Connor opened the container to find two pairs of silver tweezers, one smaller than the other. "What are these for?"

"To remove the hair from your face." She picked one up and plucked a hair off his chin, showing him how they worked.

He yelped.

"Of course, our men don't have nearly as much hair as you do," she said with a giggle. "You'd definitely create a stir in Paran if they saw it."

Connor's eyes narrowed as he rubbed the sting away. Damn silly way to shave. He'd have to find a proper razor somewhere after all this was over. "I think I'll just hold the blanket over the bottom half of my face when we reach town, if it's all the same to you."

"If anyone asks, I could tell them you're not able to talk, then you stay covered."

"That's fine, as long as I don't have to use these tortuous things." He closed the box and handed it back to Bethany. "Do we have everything we need?"

Bethany nodded.

Connor took her by the hand. "Good. Now, let's get out of here before another ice storm hits."

Bethany and Connor moved through the Digger's camp as the sun began its ascent through the sky. "Do you think the Eitellans are nearby?" she asked.

"I don't know. Those guards scattered all too quickly yesterday, even if my gun scared them. I'd also imagine the two I wounded are itching for a fight." He scanned the horizon, his mouth set in a grim line. "My guess is that this High Priestess of theirs will be plenty angry and will most likely send out an even bigger group after us."

Bethany agreed. "You're probably right. We need to get to Paran as soon as possible."

"How far did you say it is?"

"About half a day's journey, to the west," she gestured with her chin.

"Let's get a move on, then," Connor said as he picked up his pace. "I'm sure your friend's help will enable us to find Sarah that much sooner." He glanced at her as she rushed to match his long stride with her shorter one. Her long blonde hair floated out behind her like a cloud. Her cheeks were rosy from the cool air and brisk walk.

Her beauty entranced him. He surely had been in a drunken stupor when he'd first met her, not to notice that. Then again, she *had* appeared in the form of an angel. Yes, she was a beautiful woman, but her strength and spirit amazed him—made his heart constrict in his chest.

Oh, Lord, I hope everything turns out all right. I hope we find Sarah healthy and unharmed…

He also hoped that Ian Johns—Bethany's so-called family friend—would not challenge him over Bethany.

THE SUN WAS high overhead when Bethany and Connor reached the outskirts of Paran. A small town, it consisted of about two hundred families and a square containing shops where goods could be bought and sold.

"I expected your towns to be different than where I come from," Connor commented, scanning the area from their perch in the hills surrounding the town. "If I didn't know any better, I'd almost think I was back home."

Bethany began her descent down the slight hill, Connor following closely behind. "How are our buildings different from yours?" she asked as she walked, her Digger curiosity aroused.

"Well, in the west, the homes would be built mostly of wood, though some of the settlers use stone, like you have here. And, they have a pitched roof, for drainage and storage above, like this." He made a triangular shape by putting his fingertips together and spreading his arms apart. "It looks like yours are constructed almost entirely of stone with flat shale roofs." As they moved closer, he added, "We do have long porches on the fronts, though, like you."

As they entered Paran, several women hurried toward Bethany. Connor turned his back to them, drawing the blanket up over his face.

"Bethany, we're so very sorry to hear about little Sarah," one cried.

"Truly a tragedy to lose a child," another added, shaking her head.

Bethany cringed. "I haven't lost her yet," she said, gritting her teeth. She knew the women were only being kind, but she still refused to believe Sarah was dead.

"It's all right, Bethany. It takes time to adjust," one of the women said as she approached Bethany from behind, placing her arm over her shoulder.

She turned around. It was Mara, Ian's mother. "So I imagine, Mara. But I truly believe we'll find her soon."

"I understand you have to keep faith for a little while. You'll know when the time is right to let go."

Bethany considered the woman for a moment. "Tell me, have any more children disappeared? Before I left Paran, Father told me a few of the beggars were missing."

Mara nodded slowly as the other women drew closer. "The last of the ragamuffins vanished just last night. She always stayed near my house as I feed her. But she didn't come by to see me."

"Do you think she just wandered off? Maybe she found someone else to take care of her."

"I don't think so. I've looked all around town today while I shopped. I'm the only one who takes care of her." Mara shivered.

"What's happening, Bethany? Can you use the Knowing to tell us?" another woman asked.

"Yes, Bethany. Can you tell us what you see?" She clutched the baby she carried against her breast. "I fear for my own child."

Bethany took the woman by the hand. With the other, she gently caressed the baby's head. "All I can tell you right now is to keep your children close by. There's a force out there greater than we could imagine and it wants our babies."

The women gasped. "Do you know what it is? Is there anything we can do?"

Bethany shook her head. "Please, don't ask. I can't say right now. Just know that I will see it ended soon."

Mara patted Bethany on the arm. "May the Mother of All keep you safe in this battle."

Bethany smiled warmly at the woman. "Thank you, Mara." She looked through the crowd to where Connor was hanging back behind them. Their eyes met and she smiled at him.

"Who is that?" Mara asked. "I don't remember seeing him around here before. Who are you, Son?"

"He can't speak, Mara. His, um, tongue was ripped out and his mouth mangled when he was attacked by a woolet."

"A woolet, you say? I didn't know there were any around these parts."

"There aren't. I mean, he's not from here. He's from Vaydah." She took a deep breath, trying to relax as she concocted the story of Connor's origins. "His name is Connor. He's a good friend of mine. We met on a dig."

"I don't remember Ian mentioning any Connor from Vaydah."

Bethany felt Mara's eyes bore through her. "Really, Mara, I do go on digs without Ian. You know I travel with the group from Vaydah sometimes."

"Mmm. I suppose." She let her gaze move from Connor and back to Bethany. "Well, as I said before, I wish you success on your journey. I hope you do find Sarah."

Bethany hugged the woman. "Thank you, Mara." Since her own mother had died so long ago, Mara had always been there for her. She knew the woman's concern was out of love, in spite of her nosiness. "I appreciate your words."

Mara patted Bethany on the back before releasing her. "Come along, ladies," she bade her friends, "and leave Bethany to her work."

"Mother's blessings on you," they called as they walked away, throwing curious glances at Connor.

Bethany let out a long sigh. Connor stepped closer to her. "Do you think they believed me?" she asked.

"Hell, I even believed you and I knew you were lying."

His eyes crinkled at the corners and Bethany knew he was smiling at her. She fought the urge to touch him, afraid someone may be watching. It wouldn't do to have rumors swirling about them.

"Tell me, what's the big deal about me being here anyway?" he asked. "I thought this 'crossing the planes' was commonplace."

"No, it's not really," she replied. "I didn't even know for sure it could be done until I visited the Weaver, Maud Hekate. She's the one who sent me to Zachariah." Bethany glanced around to make sure no one was listening. "And she made me promise I wouldn't discuss it with anyone."

"Your secret is safe with me. I certainly don't want to be the one to tell."

As they spoke, Bethany's home came into view. "Look! There's my house! Come on!" she called as she picked up the pace.

It'll be so good to see Papa again.

She crossed her fingers, hoping he'd have some word of Sarah the women hadn't known about.

Bethany reached the front porch as Abraham stepped out from the side of the house where he'd been working. "Papa!" Bethany ran to him, arms outstretched.

"My daughter!" Abraham embraced her tightly. "Where have you been these past ten days? I thought I'd lost you, too." He held her out at arm's length, assessing her appearance. "Look at you." He shook his head. "You've lost weight. Come inside and I'll fix you something to eat."

"Wait, Papa, here's someone I want you to meet. Connor Jessup, this is Abraham Stendi, my father."

Connor seemed to hesitate, pulling the blanket tighter around his mouth.

"It's all right Connor," she smiled, motioning for him to let it down. Abraham took a step back as Connor let the blanket drop to his shoulders.

"I've never seen someone with hair so dark. What is he doing here?"

"He's a friend, come to help us find Sarah." She turned to Abraham and wrapped her arm around his. "Let's all go in, Papa. I have so much to tell you, I don't know where to begin."

CHAPTER TWENTY-FOUR

"Eitel isn't the long dead religion we thought it was. I wouldn't have believed it myself, Papa, if I hadn't seen it with my own eyes." Scooping up one final spoonful of the hearty, meaty stew, Bethany sat back in her chair. "They actually exist in this time and place."

Abraham shook his head. "Who would have thought it could happen?" His eyes filled with tears, as he placed his hand on top of hers. "And they stole our butterfly. What are we going to do?"

Bethany stared past Abraham and Connor, her sight fixed on the totem of her child that now supported one end of the fireplace mantel.

Papa must've carved that while I was gone. He believes she's dead.

"Is that Sarah?" Connor asked.

"Yes," she whispered. She turned her attention to her father. "You did a fine job on Sarah's totem, Papa. I only wish you hadn't gone to so much trouble. You should have waited until we were certain what happened to her before making it."

"But I wanted to carve it while her features were still fresh in my mind." His voice grew wispy. He stood and went to the mantel. "Why, look at the eyes. They're always the hardest to do, but this looks exactly like our baby." Abraham ran his hand gently over the wood. "I think I got the color right, too. What do you think, Daughter?"

"You did, Papa," Bethany whispered.

"Angel, are you all right? Can I get you something to drink?" Connor asked.

"Over by the fire there's a pitcher of bitters. I'd like some, please."

As Connor picked up the pitcher, Abraham eyed him suspiciously before turning to Bethany. "What'd he call you? Angel?"

"It's a pet name, Papa. Like you calling Sarah 'butterfly'."

"Well, I don't like it. It sounds *too* familiar to me. Just how well do you know this man? Where'd you meet him?" He glanced back at the other man. "And he certainly doesn't look like anyone I've ever seen before. Why just look at his strange clothes and that dark hair." Abraham leaned forward. "Where's he from?"

"Slow down, Papa." Bethany took a deep breath. This wasn't going to be easy. She might as well tell him the truth and get it over with; he'd probably figure it out eventually anyway. She *had* promised Maud not to, but how could she not explain everything to her own father?

"What I'm about to tell you, Papa, you must promise not to repeat to anyone, ever."

Connor returned with the bitters. "Bethany, are you sure about this?"

"I have to tell him; otherwise he won't leave you alone. He needs to know." She returned her attention to Abraham, who was listening intently. "Connor is a traveler from the Earth plane. I went there and asked him to come back with me to help find Sarah."

Abraham held up his hand. "Wait a moment. You're telling me he's from another world?" He shook his head. "That's not possible. It's only legend."

Bethany met his gaze straight on. "Like the Eitellans."

Abraham leaned back in his chair and crossed his arms over his chest. Taking a deep breath, he turned to Connor. "This is true, young man?"

Connor glanced at Bethany. She nodded. He looked back at Abraham. "Yes," he answered simply.

"So, tell me then, world traveler, what's in it for you?"

"I beg your pardon?"

"You heard me. If you're like most beings, you surely wouldn't venture across such a great chasm out of the goodness of your heart, now, would you?"

"Papa, please! Leave Connor be! We have more important things to discuss this evening."

"I understand, Daughter, and we will as soon as I have some

answers. Is the man not capable of speaking for himself?" He looked Connor in the eye.

Connor cleared his throat. "As a matter of fact, Sir, I did come for a specific reason other than finding Sarah."

"Ah-ha! I knew it!"

"Now hold on there a minute. You don't know the half of it. My wife, Elizabeth, left me and came to Paran and is somehow connected to these Eitellans of yours. At first I wanted to find out if she was still alive and to see her again if that was the case."

Abraham's frown turned into a scowl.

"But your daughter here cured me of an awful sickness. In the process, I was healed of my obsession with Elizabeth as well. It doesn't matter to me anymore if I see her or not. I no longer love her." Connor glanced at Bethany as he sat back down at the table. He squeezed her hand. "All that matters now is finding your granddaughter."

Abraham was quiet for a few moments, looking from Connor to Bethany and back again. "What about your feelings for my girl, here. Didn't you just say you already had a wife?"

Bethany shifted nervously in her chair. *This isn't going well at all.* "Why do you assume there are any? Connor is simply being a friend."

"I'm an old man, child. I've seen many years and I can tell if two people are in love when I'm around them." He shook his head. "You look at each other with the same light I used to look at your mother with. And I loved her with all my heart." He strummed his fingers against the arm of his chair.

"I'm sorry, Papa, but we're not prepared to discuss our feelings one way or another at the moment." Bethany's cheeks heated with her blush. "Right now, the most important thing is finding Sarah, don't you think?"

Abraham pounded his fist on the table, sending the beverage cups and bowls jumping. "Of course, it is! Do you think I'm so old I don't know what's important anymore?" He leaned over and patted her on the arm. "You've been through a great deal of pain, Daughter, and I don't want to see you hurt again." He turned his attention to Connor. "It's a father's prerogative to fret over his daughter. Wait until you have a child. You'll see."

Connor's eyes met Bethany's. "I hope I have the chance someday."

Connor's warm gaze heated her from the inside out. She smiled and gave him a small nod, then turned her attention back to her father. "If you're finished with this inquisition of yours, we'll make our plans for rescuing Sarah." She was happy Connor had stood his ground with Papa, but the questions raised concerning his wife's existence nagged at her. What if Elizabeth *were* alive? Would Connor feel the same way once he saw her again? She tamped down those worrisome thoughts.

First, find Sarah, then I can worry about Elizabeth.

As Bethany started to speak, a heavy knock sounded at the door. She rose to answer it and found Ian Johns standing there, his silhouette filling the entry. "Beth! Where in heaven's name have you been? I've been worried sick."

No doubt Mara had told him she was in town. She probably told him about the silent stranger as well. This was all she needed right after Papa's interrogation. Bethany took a step backward. "You didn't need to worry, Ian. I can take care of myself."

Ian peered over Bethany's shoulder. "May I come in? My mother told me she saw you and your friend over there in the square today. You should have sent for me," he gently scolded, his eyes on Connor.

Bethany touched his arm, diverting his attention from Connor. "I'm sorry, Ian, there wasn't time to contact you. Won't you come in?"

He started to walk past Bethany, then stopped. Ian faced her squarely, then, before she could react, took her into his arms and kissed her.

Bethany froze, first shocked by the man's action, then repelled. Her fury exploded as she shoved him away from her. "Don't ever do that again!" she spat. "What's the matter with you?"

"Bravo, lad!" Abraham called out loudly, clapping his hands. "You should have done that years ago. Maybe you two would be married by now."

Bethany sensed the hurt that ran through Ian as his eyes met hers. She wiped at her mouth and, looking away, saw Connor watching her every movement. She cringed, knowing he must be thinking the worst, but his face was set in stone—unreadable and void of emotion.

Ian walked up to Connor. "I'm Ian Johns," he offered his hand to Connor, a smug smile playing about his lips.

Connor looked at the hand, then back at Ian. "Connor Jessup. Of the Vaydah Jessups." He leaned back in the chair, stretched out his legs in front of him, and let his hand rest on the butt of his gun – a movement that wasn't lost on Bethany.

"Connor." She looked at the weapon meaningfully, remembering the encounter with Esther.

"Don't worry, Bethany. I have no intention of wasting a good bullet on this 'friend' of yours." His eyes narrowed as they caught Ian's. "Unless, of course, he forces me to."

The tension in the room was almost unbearable. Bethany kept looking from Connor to Ian, the undercurrent that ran between them a tangible emotion.

What was Ian trying to prove by kissing her like that in front of Connor?

Finally, Abraham spoke. "All right, you boys, calm yourselves down. From what Bethany tells me, Sarah may still be alive. We have a child to find and no time for your nonsense," he admonished. "You can settle your dispute over my daughter later." He turned to Bethany who smiled her thanks. "Come have a seat and tell us what we need to do."

CHAPTER TWENTY-FIVE

"**B**efore you begin, Bethany, I'd like to know more about Connor," Ian stated flatly. "You say you're from Vaydah? Well, your coloring's too dark for those people. And how did you travel that great a distance during the ice storms?" He snorted. "Everyone knows you can't travel in the ice. It's too dangerous."

Connor slowly pulled out a pocketknife, grabbed a piece of kindling from near the hearth and began hacking at it. "Let's just say where I come from, a little ice doesn't bother us too much." He looked Ian straight in the eye. "Especially if we're after something we want real bad."

Ian leaned forward. "And what might that be?"

"Figure it out for yourself," Connor gritted between clenched teeth.

"Listen, you two. Can't you put your egos aside long enough to think of Sarah?" Bethany interrupted. "My nerves are worn to a frazzle. If you don't stop it, I'll have to ask you to leave, Ian." Why did men have to be so childish? They acted as if she were their personal property.

"Me?" Ian looked up, surprised. "Why not him?" He eyed Connor. "Exactly how long have you known this man anyway, that you should choose him over me? You know how I feel about you."

"It's not a matter of choosing Connor over you, Ian. And this isn't the proper time or place to be discussing your feelings." She walked over to him and put her hand on his shoulder. "As a dear friend, I could use your help, but I won't allow you to mistreat a guest in my home."

Ian blew out a breath. "All right, Beth, if that's what you want."

"Thank you." Bethany drew up a chair and placed it near the fire.

Sitting, she warmed her hands. "Now, let me tell you what happened," she began. Then, feeling as if someone were watching her, Bethany turned slightly. Connor was staring at her and his eyes bore a hole through to her very soul. She forced herself to stay in her seat, hating the fact that she couldn't go to him and feel his arms around her right now. She turned back to the fire and related the story.

"Three days ago, while searching for clues about the Eitellans, Connor and I discovered a kiyolo. There, in the altar room, was a large statue of Yongi."

"You found the Kiyolo of Yongi? We'll have to excavate it!" Ian exclaimed. "How far away is it?"

"Near the obsidian fields," Bethany answered, smiling slightly. Maybe if she could keep Ian interested in her finds, he'd forget about Connor for a while. "I went into the Knowing and studied the statue. It was then I learned there's another kiyolo, the Kiyolo of the Night, which contains the secrets to destroying the High Priestess." She glanced at Ian and saw he was listening intently.

"But the High Priestess is immortal. She can't be killed," he interjected.

"That's what I thought, too. But according to the memories surrounding the statue, the person who would seek her power can kill her. People only think she lives forever because, with the extra years she extracts from her victims, she outlives the worshippers. The Kiyolo of the Night will tell us how to deal with her *and* save the children's souls." She looked around the table at each of the men. "It'll tell us how to rescue Sarah."

"Do you really think it's going to be that easy?" Ian asked.

Bethany sighed. "No, I don't think it'll be easy at all. We tried to find the second kiyolo but were attacked by three Eitellans."

"You actually saw them?" Abraham asked, his eyes wide. "No one has ever seen them."

"Oh, we saw them all right." She caught Connor's eye. "The leader was the same woman who took Sarah in the first place."

"The woman you saw in the Knowing?" Ian asked.

"The same." She stood and walked over to Connor. Standing behind him, she placed both hands on his shoulders. He covered her hands with his. "You've been extremely quiet during my tale. Do you have anything you want to add?"

Connor glanced at her. "Well, you didn't tell them about the Digger camp and the time we spent there." He gave a little yelp as Bethany pinched him hard on the neck.

"What about this Digger's camp?" Abraham asked, his eyes narrowed.

Before Connor could speak, Bethany answered, "There's nothing special about it, really. It's old and broken down. But it *is* located near the Kiyolo of the Night. What we need to do is gather up supplies and head there. It's about half a day's journey. We can leave for the camp in the morning, then, tomorrow night, we can sneak into the kiyolo. The moon is fully waned and won't give us away."

Ian sat back in his chair and let out a slow breath. "Sounds dangerous. I don't know if we'll be able to get anyone else to help us."

Connor leaned forward, resting his elbows on the table. He took Bethany's cup of now cold bitters and drank it down. He made a face. "My God. What's in that stuff? It tastes like pomade." He held up a hand. "No, don't tell me. I don't want to know." He stared hard at Ian. "Yes, it'll be dangerous. We have no idea how many of them are out there. My guess is if this place is so heavily guarded, it may be the High Priestess's hideout."

Bethany sat at the table. "How convenient that would be. We could take care of everything at once."

"You do have a devilish streak in you, Bethany." Connor shook his head. "So, Ian Johns, friend of Bethany, are you with us?"

Ian looked at Connor, then Bethany. He sighed. "I've been with you from the beginning, Beth. You don't have to ask."

Bethany took hold of Ian's hand. "I know, but I wanted to tell you everything, so you know what we're getting into."

"I guess I'd better head home and prepare for the morning. I'll see if I can get some of the other Diggers to come along. Maybe I can entice them with the notion of a new find."

"Don't approach anyone else, Ian. It wouldn't be fair to ask others to go into such danger. I believe, if we're smart and careful, the four of us can handle it," Bethany said. "And I don't want the possibility of anyone getting word to the High Priestess that we're going to the Kiyolo of the Night." She looked at Connor. "Do you agree?"

Connor nodded.

"Well, if that's what you want." Ian rose to leave. Bethany followed him out the door, closing it gently behind them. They walked in silence for several feet, then Ian stopped. "Why, Beth? Why him and not me?"

"It wasn't a matter of choosing. I really had no choice."

"You mean he forced himself on you? That doesn't mean you have to stay with him."

"What I meant was my heart has spoken to me." She took hold of Ian's hands. "I'll always love you, Ian, but only as a friend. I've tried to tell you that all along."

"And how do you feel about this Connor from Vaydah?"

Bethany sighed and looked into Ian's eyes. "I love him."

Ian let Bethany's hands drop. He turned and started to walk away, his shoulders sagging. "Ian, please," Bethany called after him.

He stopped and waved his hand. "It's all right, Beth. Really. I can't make you love me, can I? If Connor makes you happy, so be it." Ian looked over his shoulder. "I'll see you in the morning."

"Thank you, dear friend," Bethany whispered after him. She turned and walked back into the house to find Connor standing near the fire, studying Sarah's totem.

"She's lovely, just like you," he commented. "Your father's gone to bed. He wants you to wake him early." Connor kept his voice low so as not to disturb Abraham. He turned to face Bethany. Her eyes filled with tears. He held out his arms and she rushed into his embrace. "How'd it go out there?" He raised her chin. "When you went out that door, I was afraid you wouldn't come back to me."

"I hurt him deeply, Connor. I didn't mean to."

"We can't choose who we fall in love with, can we?"

Bethany studied his expression. Was he talking about them? She couldn't be certain. Up to now, only their bodies had spoken to each other in a language as ancient as time. No actual words had been exchanged. "Ian and I have been friends for a long time. He wanted more than I could give."

"I wasn't talking about Ian, Angel."

"No?" she swallowed hard, her heart skipping a beat.

Connor shook his head, sending his thick black hair into his eyes. Bethany reached up and brushed it away. "When you did that at the first kiyolo, that's when I knew, in here," he pointed at the center of his chest, smiling. "I just didn't realize it then."

He leaned down, his mouth so near to hers she could feel his warm breath. "And what did you come to realize?" Bethany asked, her voice a soft whisper.

"That I love you, Angel." Connor's face was serious. "We haven't known each long as far as days go, but I feel you've been with me all of my life."

Bethany stood on tiptoe, wrapping her arms around his neck, and pulled him down until their lips met. She kissed his mouth and cheeks, then his mouth again. He leaned against her, pushing her against the wall, and she could feel his need growing along with her own. "I love you, too, Connor Jessup." She made a small 'x' on her chest. "Cross my heart."

Connor laughed and scooped Bethany up, swinging her around in his arms. "Let's go to bed, Angel. I want to make love to you all night." He nuzzled her neck.

"What about Papa?" Bethany whispered. "He might hear us."

"If he does, he can cover his ears." Connor chuckled.

CHAPTER TWENTY-SIX

A t sunrise, they made their way out of Paran. Anyone watching them would most likely think they were heading to the hilltops to celebrate the winter solstice. Moving steadily eastward, they cut a narrow path, using the remaining stars as their guides.

Bethany pointed to the sky and said, "There. We need to follow the constellation Magrio. It rests over the Kiyolo of the Night." She glanced at Ian. "This was a good idea you had, disguising ourselves this way." The color choice of the robes worked well. Since the leaves were now gone, the group blended in with the bare branches. "If there are any Eitellans in town, they won't know what we're about."

They continued on in silence, pushing their way through the broadleaf forest as they headed for what they hoped would be Sarah's rescue and a confrontation with the High Priestess.

Mother of All, keep my Sarah safe just a while longer. I'm almost there.

She looked over at Connor. He hadn't left her side for a moment since last night. His presence was reassuring, and she struggled to let all doubts dissipate where Elizabeth was concerned.

I hope we find her after we find Sarah so we can end this once and for all.

"PENNY FOR YOUR THOUGHTS," Connor whispered as they walked.

"What does that mean?" She looked at him curiously.

"It means I'd pay to know what you're thinking right now."

Bethany shook her head. "Trust me, you don't want to know."

"Beth," Ian called as they entered a clearing. "The sun is rising. Why don't we stop and break our fast?" He checked the sky again. "We should only be an hour from the Digger's camp."

"That sounds like a good idea," she answered as she began to walk away from the group.

Connor placed his hand on her shoulder. "I don't think it's a good idea to wander off, Bethany," he said. "It may not be safe."

"I'm only going to say my morning prayers. I promise not to go far. I'll be right back." She turned to Abraham. "Papa, let Connor show you how he lights a fire with rocks."

"Impossible!" Abraham thumped his walking stick on the ground. He leaned toward Ian and whispered in his ear. "Thinks he can light fire with stone. Who ever heard of such a thing?"

Connor shook his head. Time to prove himself again. Frustrated Bethany had wandered off without him to say her morning prayers, he resigned himself to the fact that the woman he loved would not be told what to do.

Letting the matter drop, Connor walked to the edge of the clearing and gathered an armload of kindling and some dried leaves. Laying everything in a pile, with the sticks on the bottom and the leaves on top, he took the flint and steel from his pocket and struck a few sparks until the leaves caught on fire. He blew on them until the fire was going strong, adding some kindling as it was needed.

"Pretty handy rock you have there," Abraham commented, stroking his chin. "You bring that with you or did you find it in one of those kiyolos you and Bethany have been exploring?"

"No, I brought it with me." Connor held the flint and steel out to Abraham. "For you, Abraham." He smiled. "Perhaps it'll keep you from burning your house down."

Abraham laughed. "So, Bethany has told you about the hazards we face every time we start a fire. That's why we try to keep one burning at all times, even during the hotter months." He studied the gift. "Thank you, Connor Jessup." Walking away, Connor heard him say: "You might just be all right."

"What's that thing?" Ian asked.

"A Colt Forty-Five." Connor held it up and checked the sights, then twirled it on one finger before holstering it. He glanced at Ian out of the corner of his eyes. He appeared not to have as much confidence as last night when he strutted in and laid claim to Bethany. Poor guy, Connor thought, she must've really let him have it. "Would you like to come with me? I'm going to find a couple of bob-ears to cook."

Ian's expression lifted a bit. "All right." Together, the two men entered the surrounding woods. They weren't more than ten feet into the trees when Connor spotted a pair, side by side. In one lightning fast motion, he pulled his gun and fired two shots, striking both animals in the head. Ian jumped at the sound.

"How can you hit with such accuracy?" he asked, holding one bob-ear up by the hind legs. "You didn't even damage the pelt."

"I've had a lot of practice."

Ian stuffed the animals into a pouch. "I've never seen a weapon like that." He considered Connor for a moment. "You're not really from Vaydah, are you?"

Connor took a deep breath. Well, what would it hurt if one more person knew? His past was getting to be common knowledge anyway. "No, Ian. I'm from another plane. At least, that's the way Bethany tells it."

Ian took a step backward. "That explains everything."

"Explains what?" Connor asked, eyes narrowed.

"The way you talk, dress, the weapon you carry." He looked Connor straight in the eye, a brow raised. "Beth's fascination with you."

Connor gritted his teeth, fighting the urge to let his fist fly, when Ian jabbed at him with a finger. "Why didn't you stay where you were? Why'd you have to come to Keilah?"

With that motion, Connor swung, catching Ian in the face. Ian fell to the ground, shook his head, and jumped up again. He swung, but Connor sidestepped and only got caught on the arm. Connor returned with a punch to the stomach and Ian doubled over.

"Ian! Connor! Come quickly!" It was Abraham and he sounded desperate.

Connor started to leave, then hesitated. He sighed. "Come on,"

Connor offered Ian a hand to help him to his feet. Ian accepted it begrudgingly.

The two men hurried back to the clearing. Abraham ran up to them. "What's going on?" Connor asked.

"It's Bethany. She hasn't come back yet. Her prayers shouldn't have taken this long."

Connor glanced at the sky. He hadn't realized it but almost an hour had passed. "Gather up your belongings, Abraham. I want you to go on ahead to the camp. There's a chance Bethany might show up there. Ian and I will go looking for her in the woods."

Ian put his hand on Connor's arm. Connor looked at the hand, then at Ian. "If you're looking for another fight, it will have to wait. We need to find Bethany," Connor growled.

Ian shook his head "I wanted to apologize for picking that fight with you. I don't know what's wrong with me. I've never felt this way before."

Abraham walked over to Ian, taking in the blackened eye. "You're in love, boy. Unfortunately, she doesn't love you back." He patted him on the back. "I'm truly sorry it didn't work out between the two of you. You'd have made a fine son-in-law." He looked at Connor. "Please don't spend the rest of your days wondering what could have been if this one hadn't come along when he did. The fact is, he's here, and it seems to me she's chosen him." He bent over and picked up his pack. "I'll go to the camp now, like you said." He turned back around and Connor caught sight of a tear as it ran down his cheek.

He squeezed Abraham's arm. "I'll find her, Abraham. She probably just got carried away with her prayers for Sarah." He didn't want her father to know how worried he really was. Abraham nodded, walking away.

Connor waited until Abraham was out of sight then grabbed his pack. Throwing it over his shoulder, he turned to Ian. "Come on. I know where she may be."

Ian looked straight at Connor. "At the Kiyolo of the Night?"

Connor nodded. "That's exactly where I'm afraid she went. She is the most mule-headed woman—"

"I don't know what a mule is, but if you're comparing it to Beth, it must be extremely stubborn."

He clapped the other man on the back. "Right you are, my friend."

As they arrived at the obsidian fields, Connor pointed to the trail he and Bethany had followed a few days earlier. "That's where we were when the Eitellans found us. If you look farther that way, you can see the man-made path."

Ian nodded. "You're right. Obsidian doesn't form like that. When the volcanic ash cools, it creates long narrow streams. The first path you showed me is a more natural formation." His tone was appreciative. "You did the right thing, following this one. I don't know if I would have thought of it."

"That's the point. They hope no one thinks about it." He lowered himself onto the path, Ian following behind. "Bethany said the Eitellans always planted clumps of trees around the openings to the kiyolos, like that one over there." He raised his head and pointed to a grouping about twenty five rods from where they stood.

Ian nodded. "She's right. They also planted neighboring groups to throw people off the trail. But if this is the kiyolo's location, that would be the entrance."

Keeping low to the ground, they began their search for the kiyolo. "Keep your head down," Connor warned. "We've got to make it in without being caught this time."

CHAPTER TWENTY-SEVEN

Connor and Ian moved stealthily through the obsidian formation, each raising his head to scan the nearby land as much as he dared. "See anything?" Connor asked after Ian had finished looking around.

"Nothing. Everything's clear so far. We chose the right passage. I think I can see the entry up ahead."

They came to a low point in the chasm and got down on their hands and knees. Just as they began to crawl, a soft feminine voice called out from behind them. "Where do you think you're going?"

Slowly, the pair stood and turned around. On the ground above them was an older, auburn-haired woman wearing a long black robe, her arms crossed over her chest.

"Uh, to worship, Mistress," Ian answered. "We've come to celebrate the winter solstice."

She let her gaze run over them. "You may be wearing the pilgrim's robes, but this isn't anywhere near the hills of Paran." She smiled sweetly, pointing in the opposite direction. "You should be somewhere over there!" As she let her hand drop, five other women emerged from the entry, each carrying a cross bow.

"We've had a rush of visitors this day. So many pilgrims have taken a wrong turn it seems." She shook her head. "Take them to the pit until I have a chance to talk to High Priestess Liazar."

"One of the visitors you came across earlier wouldn't happen to be a woman, about so high?" Connor asked, holding his hand up to mid-chest height.

She shrugged. "You'll see for yourself in a few moments. Get them out of here." she commanded.

Ian started to struggle as two of the guards grabbed his arms and began to tie his hands in front of him. His eyes caught Connor's and the other man shook his head almost imperceptibly.

Ian nodded and relaxed, allowing the women to tie his wrists together as the others had done to Connor. Pulling the two men by their bindings, they led them into the bowels of the kiyolo. Descending the steps, Connor remembered another time, falling down a similar set.

If they've harmed Bethany or Sarah, I'll see them all dead.

Into the darkness they traveled, their way lit dimly by sporadic torches mounted in the sides of the cave. This kiyolo was much larger and more elaborate than the previous one Connor and Bethany had explored, with passages criss-crossing in a maze. Connor tried to keep track of each one in case they found the chance to escape, but it was useless. There were just too many.

The air was heavier and more damp which meant they were going deeper into the ground. They stopped in front of a heavy wooden door at the end of one of the corridors. It appeared to be a jail of sorts as one of the guards threw back the bar and pulled it open. Together, the women shoved Connor and Ian into the opening. Immediately, their senses were assaulted by the smell of sour urine and decay. The familiar sound of scurrying reached Connor's ears and he cringed inwardly. One of the women placed a torch into a hole in the wall, then slammed the door as she left.

Connor spied a slight form crumpled on a cot in the corner. Rushing over, he fell to his knees.

Please, God, let her be alive.

Gently, he turned her over. An ugly purple bruise covered the left side of her face. He leaned down, placing his cheek near her nose.

"Good, she's still breathing," he whispered. He glanced around the cell, spotting a bowl of water on a table in the corner. "There's a bowl of water over there. Here, soak this." He pulled a kerchief out of his shirt pocket and gave it to the other man.

Ian did as he was instructed, offering the damp rag back to Connor. "The water's pretty murky."

"It'll be all right, as long as it's cool," Connor murmured, cradling Bethany in his arms.

Rocking her back and forth, he kept the compress on the bruise.

"Wh-what happened?" she whispered.

"My God, Bethany, you had us scared."

"Where did they find you, Beth?" Ian asked.

"Connor? Ian? Where are we?"

"Some sort of jail cell in the Kiyolo of the Night. How did you get here?" Connor continued to bathe the side of her face as he spoke.

"After I said my prayers, I heard a noise behind me and when I turned, there were three women standing there. Before I could move, they attacked me." Bethany pushed herself up, then let her head drop down to her hands. "My head feels like it's full of sand."

"You've taken quite a hit. Can you heal it?"

"I can't heal myself, Connor," Bethany answered.

"Why not?" he asked.

"It's just not done. It's against the practices of a Healer to use the energy on ourselves rather than on those who would seek our aid."

"I think it's time you tried. After all, you want to be your strongest when you meet up with the infamous High Priestess, don't you?"

"The High Priestess? Is she here?"

"The woman who brought us here said something about needing to talk to the High Priestess Liazar. If she's not here, then she must be in the vicinity," Ian answered.

"If that's so, then I'll try it. For Sarah's sake," Bethany said. Slowly, she raised her hand to her head, grimacing as she gingerly felt the contusion. As she continued to run her fingertips over it, she slipped into the Knowing. A soft indigo mist formed around her head, concealing her face from view. After a few moments, she let her hands drop as her body swayed, overcome with dizziness. When the mist cleared, a shadow of the bruise was still there, but its intensity was lessened.

"You've almost done it, Bethany. Can you try again?"

Bethany felt the side of her head. The bump was there, but it was quite a bit smaller than it had been. She closed her eyes as the room began to spin and it took all of her concentration to keep from falling over the side of the cot. "I've done as much as I can. I'll be fine in a little while."

Connor lay his hand on her cheek as he leaned in to kiss her, the door opened.

"Come with me," the guard ordered, looking at Ian.

Connor stood. "We go together."

"Not this time. She wants to see him first."

"Who wants to?" Bethany asked. "Is it the High Priestess?"

"For a group of 'pilgrims,' you three seem to have a lot of questions about us," the guard snarled. Two more entered the chamber and flanked Ian.

Connor's hand moved to the gun. Ian shook his head. "Not yet. Save it. I'll be all right." Ian glanced at Bethany and smiled. "Be well, Bethany." She lifted her hand and smiled back as the guards lead him out the door.

Bethany stood and started to go to Connor when a wave of dizziness swept through her. She teetered as Connor rushed to her side. He gathered her into his arms, holding her tightly against him.

"This is my fault, Connor. Ian only came because I asked him to. She'll kill him."

"We can't know that for sure. As for Ian's being here, you couldn't have stopped him. He wants to help you find Sarah, too. He's a good man." He leaned over and kissed the top of her head. "I have a friend like him at home. He never leaves me, even when I treat him like a dog."

"A dog?" Bethany sniffed.

"Yeah, it's a small furry animal. Very loyal. Anyway, Jimmy Brown Eagle, that's his name, well I think he'd follow me to the ends of the earth. Of course, it goes both ways."

"I remember Jimmy. He's the one who was with you in the tent and at the portal, wasn't he?"

Connor grinned. "The very same."

"I'd like to meet him in person someday," she said.

"I hope you will, Angel. But right now, you need to rest." He helped her back to the small cot. Sitting down, he pulled Bethany onto his lap. She curled up in his embrace, resting her head on his chest.

"Where have you been, Billy Boy, Billy Boy? Oh, where have you been, charming Billy?" he crooned in Bethany's ear.

Bethany held tight to Connor and tears rolled down her cheeks as Ian's screams echoed around them.

CHAPTER TWENTY-EIGHT

The torch's weak flame eventually sputtered out, leaving Bethany and Connor in virtual darkness. They stayed on the cot for most of the day. Ian's yells of pain had stopped some time ago and now they kept vigil for his return. It was evening when the door finally scraped open. A thin stream of yellow light slowly expanded to fill the entire room. Bethany ran to the door.

"Ian?" she called.

A guard pushed her way in. "Move away from the door."

Bethany backed up. "Where's Ian?"

"Resting," the guard answered with a vague smile. She placed a tray of food on the floor and turned to leave.

"Excuse me, ma'am," Connor called. "Would you be so kind as to leave us a fresh torch? I'd like to make sure it's food I'm eating and not one of the varmints I keep hearing running about."

"I suppose that would be acceptable." She took the extinguished torch from its holder and replaced it with a fresh one another guard handed her. She cast a backward glance at the pair, then closed the door behind her.

Bethany carried the tray to the cot where Connor was sitting. Together, they shared the meager fare of flat bread and berries, washing it down with cold bitters. After one swallow, Connor grimaced.

"Like I said before," she said, "it takes some getting used to."

"I don't think I ever will." He shivered, swallowing the drink.

"I've been thinking, Connor. Do you suppose they used this cell for anyone who may have challenged the priestess and lost?"

Connor shrugged. "They could have. What difference would it make?"

"Well, I could go into the Knowing and see if there's any information to be found. If someone was here who knew the answer to what we seek, maybe I can find out." She chewed on a piece of the hard bread and shrugged. She looked at Connor. "What do you think?"

"If it'll help us get out of this hell hole and find Sarah and Ian, I say do it. It sounds like a good idea to me." He cleared the tray from the cot and placed it near the door. "What do you want me to do?"

"Nothing, other than try to remember whatever I tell you. I can't always recall everything I've said." She shifted to the edge of the bed, placed her feet on the floor, and went into the Knowing.

"Tell me what you see, Bethany," Connor bade quietly.

Bethany scanned the room. Generation upon generation of prisoner began to appear. Some old, some young. Men, women, children. All manner of dress and demeanor, from the richest nobleman to the lowliest slave. "There are so many people here. I can't make out what any of them are saying." She put her hands over her ears. "It's getting too loud."

"Pick out one person and shut out the others," Connor whispered as though he were in her head. "You can do it. Go slowly and seek one person at a time."

Bethany nodded. "I see a young woman. She's sitting on her heels, crying…"

"My baby, my baby," the woman sobbed. "They killed you." She rolled her eyes heavenward. "Sweet Mother of All, please forgive me for turning against you. The Eitellans offered worldly riches but they stole my child. I'd gladly give it all back to save his soul. They might as well kill me, too."

"Hasn't someone told you what we had in mind?" a voice called through the door. "Come sunset, the priestess will take you, too, though I can't see why she'd bother as old as you are." Laughter mixed with the sound of footsteps echoing down the hallway as the guard walked away.

"Oh, Connor, they took her child, too," Bethany cried. "What if we don't find Sarah? What if we're going about this all wrong?"

Connor put his arm around her shoulders and drew her close. "You've got to trust your instincts, you know that. It's what's brought us this far. Try again," he urged. "Pick out someone else."

She nodded. "There's an old woman in the corner." In her mind's eye, the woman came into clear focus. She was wearing the garb of a priestess, only it was dirty and torn. Her pewter gray hair had been shorn above her ears and all her jewelry removed. Bethany listened as she talked to herself, repeating the words in a murmur for Connor's benefit.

"Throw me in here, will you? Upstart!" She picked up a stick and started to scratch at the wall, making marks. Bethany struggled to decipher the writing. It was a type of old cuneiform, similar to what she had seen on Yongi's statue. Perhaps they were from the same time period.

"What can I do for revenge?" The old woman stroked her chin. "I know! I know!" A bony finger sliced the air. "I'll leave a message of death for future Eitellans. If I convey the secret words, then they'll be able to destroy the priestesses that follow me."

With the stick, she dug at the mortar surrounding one of the smaller blocks of which the wall was constructed. Finally, it loosened and she struggled with it until she was able to slide it out halfway. She put her hand inside one of the knee-high boots she wore, pulling out a thick, sharp skinny implement, like an oversized sewing needle. Furiously, she scratched and dug, forming the letters that would spell certain death for future priestesses.

Bethany watched in a few moments what must have taken the old woman several months to write. Every night, she'd force the block out and work. On the left side, she made the markings. On the right, she dug until a small hole was formed. When her work was finished, she placed the needle into the hole and slipped the stone into place for the last time. That night, a guard came to take her away. The old priestess never returned.

Bethany walked slowly over to the wall perpendicular to the cot. Pushing the bed out of the way, she dropped to her hands and knees and searched the stones. There it was. The one she'd seen in the vision. She sat back on her haunches. "Connor, come here."

He squatted down next to her. "Is that the stone?"

"Yes." She dug with her fingers at the sand the old priestess had packed into the joints until enough was gone to allow her to slip her hands in next to it. "I can feel the carvings," she said, sliding the stone forward.

Connor went to retrieve the torch. "Can you read it?"

"It's an old tongue but, yes, I think I can interpret it." She lay down on her stomach in order to have a better look. She ran her fingers over the letters.

"What's it say?"

"'Hear my words, children of Eitel. If you would destroy the priestess, her head she must lose. Take this gift and put it to good use. Shaken thrice, a weapon you'll have. Strike fast and sure. You'll not get a second chance.'" Bethany sat up and leaned back against the cot, crossing her arms over her knees.

"Didn't you say something earlier about the woman placing something in the stone?" Connor asked, reaching around its side. "Here it is." He pulled out the shiny silver needle and handed it to Bethany.

Bethany paced to the center of the room. "It said to shake it three times to kill the priestess. Do you think I can kill her from here?"

She gave the needle a good shake downward, but nothing happened. She shook it two more times and the instrument began to glow a bright orange. She dropped it and backed away, watching wide eyed as it stretched and grew in length.

"My God," Connor said, standing behind her. He moved past Bethany and picked it up. "It's a sword."

"Of course!" She clasped her hands together. "'If you would destroy the priestess, her head she must lose.' The High Priestess must be beheaded!"

"Beheaded?" Connor swallowed hard.

Bethany nodded. Taking the weapon from Connor, she watched as it returned to its normal size then fastened it to the inside of her blouse. "As sure as I've ever been about anything in my life."

CHAPTER TWENTY-NINE

The cell door's bar hit the stone floor with a heavy thud, cutting through the stillness of the tomb-like cell. The noise jolted Bethany and Connor awake.

Esther walked in with a guard on either side, her arm in a sling. She placed a new torch in the holder and turned to face the pair. "Well, well. We've met before, haven't we?" She eyed Connor. "I suppose you came back so I could thank you for this," she said, pointing at the injury. "You really should have stayed away when you had the chance. Now you'll have to deal with Liazar. I don't mind telling you she's in a foul mood this morning. That friend of yours kept her up all night with his howling."

"What did she do to Ian?" Bethany demanded, rising from the cot. "Tell me or I'll finish what Connor started."

"Really, *Connor*, you should keep a muzzle on this one. She'll get both of you into trouble for sure," Esther hissed.

Connor moved to stand in front of Bethany, shielding her from the other woman. Esther immediately caught sight of the gun. "Take that from him!" she commanded the women with her. "Didn't you check them for weapons?"

The two guards looked at each other sheepishly. "Yes, Ma'am. Please forgive us. We didn't know what it was. It looked like some sort of ornament." As one guard held a crossbow at Connor's throat, the other took his gun. Esther held out her hand and accepted it.

Bethany and Connor stood stock-still, unable to move with the arrows pointing at them, waiting as the guards checked their persons for anything else they may have. Satisfied they didn't possess any other weapons, they stepped away. Bethany allowed herself a small sigh of relief. They hadn't found the needle.

Esther smiled at Connor. "She's especially interested in you, dear sir."

"Why?" Connor's eyes narrowed.

"No idea but I suppose you'll find out soon enough." Esther stepped to the side as the guards shoved the pair in front of them. Holding a crossbow at each of their backs, they directed Bethany and Connor down the long winding corridor to meet with the High Priestess, Liazar.

BETHANY FORCED herself to take slow, deep breaths as they moved down the dark, musty corridor. She was thankful she and Connor were being taken together. His strength would help keep her from losing her resolve.

Soon, Sarah, soon. Mama's coming.

Connor whispered in her ear. "We'll get through this, Bethany."

"I love you," she whispered back. "No matter what happens, please know that."

"I love you, too." He cleared his throat. "Damn, I can't help but feel like we're being led to the gallows."

"Gallows?"

"Never mind. It's an unpleasant place."

"You two be quiet." Esther called from behind them. "We're here."

They stopped in front of a large wooden door as wide as the corridor. Esther pushed past them and knocked at it first twice, then a pause, then another four times.

Slowly the door creaked open. They had to cover their eyes because of the brightness of the room. Everywhere, torches glowed. Esther motioned for the guards to proceed and they pushed Bethany and Connor forward.

As her eyes grew used to the light, Bethany noticed they were in an altar room, but it was unlike any she had ever seen. At least four times the size of the usual ones she helped to excavate, it extended well beyond the entry. The walls were painted similarly to Yongi's kiyolo, with further tales of the life of Eitel. At the center of the room was an immense white marble throne instead of a statue.

When they were within ten feet of the seat, Esther ordered them to stop. "That'll be far enough."

From somewhere inside the altar room, the sweet melody of a lyre floated out to them. As the musician strummed, a woman with long, dark red hair emerged from behind the throne and took her seat. She let her gaze pass over Bethany and come to rest on Connor.

"My God." Connor gasped.

"It's been a long time, dear Connor. Is that all you have to say to your wife?"

Elizabeth?

Bethany's mind reeled. The two women she had grown to despise were one and the same. She looked from Connor to Elizabeth, unable to speak.

"I thought you were dead," Connor said, his voice low.

Elizabeth eyed Bethany. "So, it would seem."

Connor drew himself up. "What have you done to yourself? You look like hell."

She pounded a fist on the arm of the throne. "On the contrary. I'm the picture of health, thanks to the hospitality of these delightful Eitel-lans." She flung her long red tresses over her shoulders.

"What I meant was, any trace of my *former* wife is completely gone," Connor spat. "You may appear beautiful on the outside, but I know your insides are rotten to the core. You've sold your soul to the Devil himself."

Elizabeth scowled and leaned forward. "I see you haven't lost your self-righteous do-gooder ways. I happened to arrive during one of their celebrations. I stepped out of a kiyolo and there they were. Well, you can imagine what must have been running through their minds to see someone appear in such a way." She leaned back, resting her head against the cold stone. "Seems the priestess who preceded me wasn't too popular. I'd read the Book of Eitel and knew how to get rid of her.

So, I did. And I took her place" She studied her fingernails. "Fascinating story, don't you think? They even gave me a new name. *Liazar.*" She waved her hand in the air. "It means rebirth."

Bethany took a deep breath, forcing herself to stay calm. "So, you're Elizabeth?" she asked, her voice tinged with sarcasm. "Really, Connor, whatever did you see in her to make her your wife?"

Elizabeth's eyes flashed sparks of anger and her hands gripped the armrests of her throne.

Good. I've rattled her.

Bethany was glad for the hidden sword. When the time was right, she would strike.

Elizabeth turned back to Connor. "Dear *husband*, what brings you here? I wouldn't have thought you could have climbed out of that whiskey bottle long enough to figure out how to cross over."

He shrugged and pointed his chin toward Elizabeth's hand. "I see you're still wearing the ring I gave you."

Elizabeth held up her hand and studied the sparkling gemstones in the candlelight. "It is quite lovely. I couldn't bear to part with it."

Bethany sensed Connor's tightly leashed tension. She shifted closer to him, her fingers lightly brushing his.

Be strong my love. We'll get through this.

"Didn't Michael give you a new one?" Connor said in a bland tone.

"He didn't live long enough."

"The ashes from the dig," Bethany whispered. "They must have been his…"

Elizabeth gave a deep sigh. "Dear Michael. I had to kill him. He wasn't interested in joining me in overthrowing the old high priestess and I couldn't have him working against me." She flicked a glance at Bethany. "You must have been part of the expedition that found my little treasure. You didn't really think the remains were mine, did you?"

Bethany and Connor turned at the sound of heavy footsteps behind them.

"Ian!" Bethany screamed, running to him. He smiled weakly and dropped to the floor. His shirt was torn and bloody, his body covered with cuts and bruises. Bethany knelt at his side. Slowly, she turned back to face Elizabeth. "What did you do to him?"

"Just looking for some information. And this." She displayed the silver box Ian had found not so long ago. "Seems he's been taking care of it for me."

Bethany turned back to Ian. She took a deep breath and shifted into the Knowing. Raising her hands, she placed them on his shoulders and began to knead them, easing the soreness away.

"What's she doing?" Elizabeth called in a sharp tone.

"She's a Healer, my Priestess," Esther explained.

"A Healer? Make her stop!"

Esther gave Bethany a shove and broke her concentration. She shook her head to clear it, then turned back to Elizabeth. "You evil woman."

Elizabeth threw her head back and laughed. "A healer. I could use the soul of a healer," she murmured. "Come, stand before me."

Bethany stayed where she was.

Elizabeth continued to eye her. "I said come here!" One of the sentries gave Bethany a rough shove from behind, sending her sprawling to the floor. Connor growled and moved to go to her but two of the guards flanked him, shoving their bows into his sides.

"It's all right," Bethany said to Connor as she stood. The sentry pushed her forward again, forcing her to stand directly in front of Elizabeth.

"You're quite beautiful and still reasonably young," Elizabeth observed.

Bethany's eyes narrowed. "What have you done with the children of Paran? Where's my daughter?"

"Daughter?" Elizabeth tapped her fingers on her cheek, thinking. "Oh yes, that explains why you look so familiar. The cherub does favor her mother, I see." Elizabeth smiled.

Bethany lunged for her, screaming, "I want Sarah! Give her to me!"

Connor took advantage of Bethany's attack to turn on the two guards flanking him. Before they could react, he threw two punches and they toppled to the floor, unconscious.

"Here, my Priestess!" Esther yelled, pulling the gun out of her sling and tossing it to Elizabeth. "It's a weapon."

Connor made a grab for her, but it was too late. Elizabeth caught the gun. Connor punched Esther in the jaw, sending the woman reeling to the ground.

"I know what it is," Elizabeth replied through gritted teeth as she fought Bethany. She kicked Bethany and scrambled for the gun where it had landed on the floor. Sitting up she pointed the gun at Bethany.

"No!" Ian screamed, making a dive for Elizabeth. Before Bethany could react, Elizabeth turned the gun on Ian and shot him in the chest. He dropped to the ground in a broken heap, blood pooling beneath him.

Connor and Bethany rushed to his side. Bethany laid her hands on his chest and tried to heal him, but it was too late. His spirit had departed.

Connor stood and turned to his wife. "Why, Elizabeth? Why did you come here?"

"After Michael presented me with the Book of Eitel, I discovered a power unsurpassed. A power so great it has made me immortal. I'll live forever here." She spread her arms wide. "Look at me, Connor. I've hardly aged. And look at my hair." She lifted the tresses and let them fall back down. "It flows with the life of all the souls I've taken."

"I always knew you were a little crazy, but I never thought you were capable of murder."

Bethany slowly rose, extracting the needle from inside of her blouse at the same time. With three quick downward thrusts, it grew into a sword. The sword she'd use to kill this woman.

Elizabeth eyed Bethany as she approached the throne. "You can't kill me with your toy. Don't you know I'm immortal?"

"Save it for the worshippers, Elizabeth. I've seen the writings. I *know* you can die." She aimed the point at her, then raised it. As she did so, Elizabeth leveled the gun.

"No!" Connor yelled, rushing forward. Just as he reached Bethany, Elizabeth fired. He shoved Bethany out of the way and caught the bullet in his thigh. He hit the hard floor with a thud as the bullet passed through, tearing the muscle.

"Connor," Bethany cried running to his side.

"Give me the sword," he ground out.

Bethany opened her mouth to argue as Connor stood unsteadily. "I'll see this through. It's my battle, Bethany."

"It's both of ours, Connor. She has Sarah." Bethany raised the sword once more and approached Elizabeth. She took two steps before the other woman fired the gun again.

The force of the bullet as it hit her shoulder knocked Bethany to the ground. She dropped the sword with a loud clatter.

"Bethany!" Connor went to her and checked the wound. Groaning with relief he whispered to her to stay down. He reached for the sword and limped toward Elizabeth.

"This is ridiculous, Connor." Elizabeth chuckled.

He gripped the sword tightly in his hands.

I can't believe I ever thought I loved this woman.

His thoughts shifted to Bethany, so loving, so brave. Her beauty shone from within.

"Why not join me here. You can be immortal, too," she purred.

"Not at the expense of other's lives," he stated flatly. Connor lifted the sword.

"You won't do it," she taunted. She raised the gun once more and fired, catching Connor in the forearm. He stumbled slightly and almost dropped the sword. But the sight of Bethany, where she lay in her own blood, spurred him on. In one swift motion, before Elizabeth could shoot the gun again, the sword flew through the air and sliced through her fine-boned neck, sending her head tumbling down the steps of the throne.

Her body twitched and a sudden rush of air flew out of her open neck, carrying all the souls she had taken. Glowing golden in the torch-light, they rushed and squealed, circling the room, delighting in their newfound freedom. He watched in amazed silence as they slipped, one after another, through a small opening in the floor behind the throne.

He started to follow them, but Bethany moaned, and he returned his attention to her.

"Heal yourself, Bethany. You did it before. You can do it again," he urged as he tied his kerchief around his wounded thigh.

"I'm so tired," she murmured.

"I'm here. Use my strength." Connor took her hand. "Please, Angel, I need you. I love you."

Bethany closed her eyes and Connor watched as a warm pink glow began to emanate from her body. It enveloped the wound, stopping the blood flow and making the skin new again. She slowly sat up, holding her head until she felt able to move. "You're hurt, too. Let me—" she reached for him, but he brushed her hand away.

"I'll be fine. They're only flesh wounds."

She touched his cheek and nodded. "Did you hear something?" she asked, looking around the room.

Connor shook his head. "What did it sound like?"

Bethany didn't answer but stood shakily and followed the noises. Reaching the back of the throne, she gave it a hard shove. It slid forward. Standing on the stairs were several small forms, scrambling toward the light. One in particular stood out, her long silver-blonde hair illuminated by the fire of the torches.

"Momma!" Sarah cried, rushing into her mother's outstretched arms.

"Oh, baby." Bethany fell to her knees, tears streaming down her face, and embraced her child. "Don't ever leave me again."

CHAPTER THIRTY

Connor was silent as he and Bethany approached the portal between the planes. "Penny for your thoughts," Bethany echoed his words.

He smiled. "I was just thinking about Abraham when he saw Sarah. I've never seen a man as happy as he was."

"Papa spoils her too much." She sighed. "I used to scold him about it, but I think I'll let him be from now on." She kicked at a rock as they crossed the almost barren land. With winter upon them, the trees and bushes were dormant for the season, their branches laid bare. It was cold enough now for the ice to stay on the ground and they stepped carefully. Bethany shivered and pulled her heavy shawl more tightly around her.

Connor removed his own jacket and draped it around her shoulders as they walked. Abruptly, he stopped and doubled over, a grimace crossing his face.

"What is it?" Bethany asked, her brow wrinkled with worry.

Connor took a deep breath and straightened. "It's nothing."

Bethany eyed him. "Don't lie to me, Connor Jessup. Let me help you." She pushed the long sleeves of the coat out of her way and raised her arms to him.

"I said I'm all right, Bethany." He winced again. "Really."

"Promise me you'll say something if it gets any worse."

"Cross my heart."

"I wish you didn't have to leave."

"I won't be gone long but I've got to let Elizabeth's and Michael's families know what's become of them—in a round-about way that is."

He stopped as they reached the wall of shale. "I feel I owe it to them. Besides, I need to say good-bye to Jimmy."

"I understand," Bethany replied softly. "Zachariah?" she called out, searching the wall. Ah, there it was—the blue glow.

"I'm not telling any fortunes today," Zachariah boomed from within the mountain.

Bethany laughed. "I seek no fortunes, Sir, only a moment of your time for two weary travelers."

The ground vibrated as the crack in the side of the mountain slowly opened, allowing entry to the portal. Hand in hand, Bethany and Connor passed through the opalescent haze. There, on the other side, Zachariah waited, his arms outstretched.

"Bethany M'Doro and Connor Jessup!" he greeted them. "I didn't expect to see you two again so soon."

"We did it, Zachariah. We found Sarah."

Zachariah clapped his hands together. "Wonderful! I told you your mission was blessed. Come, sit by the fire. I have someone here who'd love to hear your tale."

Bethany and Connor walked toward the fire. Sitting with her back to them was the slight, bent form of a woman. She turned around, her eyes dancing. "Maud!" Bethany exclaimed. "What are you doing here?"

"Visiting an old friend." She smiled at Zachariah. "He told me of your journey as a shadow." She patted the chair next to her. "Sit, child, and tell me your story. I need some new tales to weave."

Connor whispered to Bethany. "Who is she?"

"Maud Hekate, this is Connor Jessup." She beamed at the man beside her. "My husband."

"Husband! Well, well, much *has* happened," Zachariah observed with a sly smile.

And so, Bethany and Connor sat near the fire. Sipping a cup of bitters, Bethany told them about the search for the Eitellans, the destruction of Liazar, and the release of the souls. More importantly, she told them of Sarah's homecoming and her wedding to Connor. It was a simple ceremony in the woods near her home. Abraham and

Sarah were there to witness the declaration of their love and commitment to each other.

As Bethany spoke, Maud strummed the air, creating and refining the fabric of color she'd use to relate the story to others later. Connor sat, transfixed. "How do you do that?"

"It's a gift I received from my father. He received it from his mother before him and so on."

"Fascinating," he whispered.

"There's one thing, though, that I still haven't been able to figure out about all of this," Bethany began. "How did the Book of Eitel come to be on the Earth plane in the first place?"

Maud finished her weaving and inspected the texture and construction of the display before her then turned back to Bethany. "When I was young, my father told me a story about his grandmother. She was an Eitellan who lived in fear of the day the High Priestess would demand her children. She stole the Book and hid it on the island where I now live. Do you remember when I told you my mother was from Earth?"

Bethany nodded.

"When she heard the stories, she feared the sect would become active again. It was she who took the Book and left it on Earth."

"And Elizabeth found it." Bethany shook her head, amazed at the chain of events that had brought her to this point.

Connor put down his cup. "It's time I left."

"Where's he going?" Zachariah asked.

"He's returning to Earth for a time. He needs to mend the fabric of his old life before he begins anew," she explained.

Connor stood and pulled her to her feet. They embraced. "Be sure and listen for him, Zachariah. He'll be back soon," she said, tears streaming down her face.

Together, arm in arm, they made their way to the point of crossing. Reluctantly Bethany released her hold on him. Passing through the portal, he turned and waved. "I love you," Bethany called. She stared for a long time into the passageway after he had gone.

She finally turned around when Zachariah placed a hand on her shoulder. "Why didn't you tell him about the child?" he asked, his voice low.

Bethany hugged her arms about her middle. "I didn't want him to feel he couldn't return to Earth if that's what he wanted. But I will tell him, Zachariah." She smiled sadly. "The next time he dreams."

EPILOGUE

Bethany sat in front of the fire, contemplating the flames as they shifted about. Red, blue, orange—images formed, then disappeared again. She let her gaze wander around the dark room as the shadows reached out. A chill ran up her spine, a sense of foreboding filling her heart.

"Connor, my love, will you ever return?" she wondered aloud. Eight months had passed since he'd left and still there was no sign of him. Bethany had stayed on for a while at Zachariah's after Connor returned to Earth. She spent the time visiting with him and Maud and using the portal to communicate with her husband. She would have liked to return again to see what was delaying Connor but was too far along in her pregnancy to travel the distance safely.

Don't worry. He'll be home as soon as he's able...

Suddenly, Bethany clutched her stomach as a sharp pain tore through her, taking her breath away. She shifted in the chair, trying to find a comfortable position.

She stared back into the fire, welcoming its comfort, but longing for something more. Then, a dark image filled her mind. "No," she whispered, fighting the vision that clouded her sight. "No!" She screamed the word this time, jumping from the chair.

Abraham threw open his bedroom door and hurried to her. "What is it, Daughter? Is it time for the child to come?"

Bethany fell to her knees, her eyes never leaving the hearth. She wrapped her arms around her shoulders, rocking back and forth as she sobbed. "Sweet Mother. He's gone, Papa." She looked up into his face, the tears streaming down her cheeks. "Connor's dead."

"How can that be? Are you certain?"

Bethany fell forward as another contraction wracked her body. Abraham helped her to her feet, guiding her into the bedroom. "I saw him. He was in bed. His friend was at his side," she cried. "I watched his last breath, Papa. I saw his soul as it drifted away. I knew he wasn't well when he left. I shouldn't have let him go. What am I going to do?"

Abraham hugged his daughter, tears welling in his eyes. "He needed to go to his home one last time. You couldn't have prevented it, as much as I know you would've liked to." He patted her stomach. "We'll figure out what to do later. Right now, I think you need to concentrate on having this child."

He looked over and found Sarah standing in the doorway, rubbing her eyes. "Is Mama all right?" she asked sleepily. "I heard her crying."

Abraham went to her side and knelt down so his eyes were level with hers. "She's going to be fine, Butterfly. But right now, she's going to have your little brother or sister." He placed his hands on her shoulders. "I need you to go to Cinda the Birther and let her know it's your mama's time to deliver. Can you do that for me?"

Sarah nodded, smiling. "Of course, I can."

Bethany moaned as another contraction came upon her. "Please hurry, Sarah." She held her breath for a moment. "The pains are coming more quickly now."

FOR THE REMAINDER of the night, Bethany fought against the image of Connor's death. Maybe she had misinterpreted it. Maybe he was fine and she was only seeing someone else who happened to look like her husband. But deep down, Bethany couldn't deny it and knew what she had seen was true. She recalled Zachariah's words from the hall of the Akashic Records. "He leaves the Earth plane in 1875." 1875. That was the year she found him and the year he returned. Grief ripped through as deep as the pain of giving birth.

Bethany struggled to relax, knowing it would ease the babe's delivery, but it was to no avail. With Cinda at her side, the cries of a new child finally echoed throughout the house in time to greet the rising sun. The Birther presented the baby to Bethany and fussed over it for a time, making certain all was well before she left.

"I'll be back tonight to check on you," Cinda called as she left the room.

Abraham and Sarah waited at the doorway and, as the woman left, rushed to Bethany's side. "He's a fine-looking boy," Abraham said proudly. "Looks a bit like me, don't you think? Except for that head of black hair, that is."

"Oh, Mama, he's beautiful. What are we going to call him?"

Bethany caressed Sarah's cheek with the back of her hand. "What do you think of Ian, in memory of our friend."

"Ian." Sarah considered the name. "I like it just fine." She leaned into the baby's face. "Hello, Ian. I'm your sister Sarah."

Bethany smiled, touched by her daughter's words. But the smile quickly faded. "Oh, Papa."

Abraham sat down on the bed. "Sarah, it's time for you to get some rest now. You can visit with your mama and new brother later."

Sarah made a face and started to argue but Abraham gave her a hard stare. She shrugged her shoulders, kissed everyone, then scurried off to her room.

Returning his attention to Bethany, he took her hand into his. "I'm so sorry, Daughter. But I know you'll manage just fine the same as before when you lost Joseph." He shook his head. "I only wish there was something I could do."

"Your being here with me is a comfort, Papa. Thank you."

Hearing a soft knock at the front entry, Abraham rose to answer the door. Bethany lay back and fell into an exhausted sleep, nuzzling her new son in the crook of her arm. She stirred when she felt one side of the bed lower, as if someone were sitting next to her. Slowly, she opened her eyes.

"I must be dreaming," she murmured to the baby. "It looks like your father is here with me." She closed her eyes again, a single tear running down her cheek. "Sweet Mother, isn't it enough that you have my husband and my heart? Please don't torment me so."

"She's not, my love."

Bethany's eyes flew open. "Connor! B-but, how?"

He reached out and caressed her cheek, then smiled at his son. "May I?" he asked, holding his arms out.

Mutely, Bethany handed the child over. "I saw you die," she whispered, overcome with tears. "I saw your soul leave your body."

"I'm so sorry I didn't come sooner. You have to believe I wanted to desperately, but there was such pain." He closed his eyes tightly. "It felt like my gut was being torn open. I couldn't get out of bed and spent most of my time not even knowing what was going on around me."

"Oh, Connor," Bethany whispered, her voice ragged.

"Yesterday was real strange, though. The pain turned into a fog and shrouded my entire being. The next thing I knew, I felt myself lifting off the bed. I saw a bright white light and headed toward it. I thought maybe it was the portal." Connor smiled warmly at Bethany. "Then I was stopped by a woman. Before I knew what was happening, she escorted me to your door. When she left, I found this sitting on the ground next to me." Connor held out a basket, offering it to her.

Bethany peered into the basket. Her eyes filled with tears and she smiled at her husband.

It was filled with Paran's Love.

A NOTE FROM THE AUTHOR

I hope you enjoyed *Shadow Dreams*, Book 2 in the Oracle Dreams Trilogy. If you'd like to leave a review, please visit Amazon.com.

I love to hear from readers! You can contact me through my website at www.teribarnett.com. While you're there, please go ahead and subscribe to my newsletter so you can stay up to date on new releases, special offers, and giveaways.

And, for a special treat, keep reading for a Sneak Peek of *Pagan Fire*, Oracle Dreams Trilogy: Book 3!

SNEAK PEEK
PAGAN FIRE
ORACLE DREAMS TRILOGY: BOOK 3

Tintagel, Cornwall, Isle of Great Britain
November 865 A.D.

"'Tis a fine night for a child to be born," Manfred cu Llwyr whispered, lost in thought as he warmed himself before the robust fire which burned brightly there. Shaking himself out of his reverie, he strode to the thick oak and iron door that led outside.

Opening it with a loud scrape, he made his way down the unheated corridor. As he moved, his body cast shadows tall and thin before him from the glow of torches mounted high on the wall. The straw scattered about the stone floor for warmth and cleanliness offered a muffled crackle beneath his feet.

Once out of doors, he rubbed his hands together and raised his eyes to the sky. On the horizon, the setting sun cast a red glow and turned the gray winter clouds to indigo. Manfred sighed and his breath hung in the air before him.

He stopped near another fire—one of many lit this night in celebration of the feast of Samhain—and leaned against the timber and stone wall of the keep. He looked out past the fence—hand-hewn stakes of wood sunk deep in the ground—surrounding his *burh*. A fine mist hovered about the treetops, its long fingers beginning to touch the ground.

It all belonged to him. As far as the eye could see, from the lush green rolling hills to the thick forests shaded dark by the coming night. The sharp tang of the sea, not quite a mile away, rose on the wind and tickled his nose.

The Samhain bonfires scattered along the hillsides broke the shroud of mist and night. His churls would soon be starting the dedication of animal sacrifices to the gods, goddesses, and denizens of the Otherworld. It was their sincere belief these offerings would cause the deities to look upon the people favorably and see them safely through the coming winter.

He hoped their prayers would be heard, thankful the portents hadn't indicated a harsh winter on the way. If this had been the case, a human sacrifice would have been in order. And though it would've been his duty to see it through, he was loath to take a life.

Manfred's "new way of thinking" was a constant point of contention between himself and the High Council of Bards, Ovates, and Priests. It was even worse with his twin brother, Eugis, who saw Manfred's beliefs as a threat to their very way of life.

A woman's scream pierced the growing darkness and Manfred swung around. He let his breath out slowly, clenching his fists until his nails dug deep in the callused flesh. Nestled deep inside the hall in their bedchamber, his wife was laboring to bring forth their first child. He unclenched his hands and cast a log on the fire in front of him. Silently, he sent a prayer to Nuada for Rhea's safety.

By the gods, he was fearful of losing her. She had come into his life like a bright shining light, at a time when he thought love was perhaps beyond his grasp, and she enchanted him. She was truly a child of the hills, with her thick black hair and freckled cheeks. She wove wondrous stories of meetings with the Tuatha de Danaan themselves, the very fays who lived in these emerald hills! And who was he to dispute her? He'd seen enough of magic in his own life to know it existed.

Lost in his thoughts, he didn't notice the little boy approaching. The child stopped before him and tugged at Manfred's long white tunic. The copper and stone adornments chimed together. The movement startled him, and he glanced down. He'd forgotten he was still wearing the heavily embroidered and jeweled priest's robes. As the Chief Dyrrwed Bard for his clan, he should be at the Samhain celebration now, reciting the stories of the Ulster Men, Cu Chulainn, and the other heroes and deities.

Ah, but he couldn't leave Rhea's side for long as she struggled with the birth. If only for his own sense of well-being, he needed to be close to her. Too many women died while laboring. He would stay and make certain the midwife and priestess in attendance drew upon all of their powers to keep his wife safe from harm while the baby fought its way into the world. And a fight it truly was. Already a full day had passed and still the babe remained in its mother's womb.

"Dylan mac Connall. What is it?" Manfred squatted down to be eye level with the boy. "What can I do for you this evening?"

The boy didn't answer, but only watched the older man.

"I would've thought you'd be at the feast with the others." Manfred smiled as he looked at the child. Hair as black as the night sky and eyes to match, the boy was so serious for one who'd seen only four winters. But he'd always been that way. Even as a wee babe he didn't cry out or raise his voice. He only seemed to look out on creation with sober curiosity.

Dylan pursed his lips together, then spoke. "I told Da I needed to be here with you and the Lady. He said it would be all right, as long as I didn't get in anyone's way." Dylan's father, Fox mac Connall, was the leader of the neighboring lands and Manfred's oldest and most trusted friend.

Manfred smiled again and ruffled the boy's hair. "But the festivities have only just begun. Have you had your fill of our good cook Hazel's honeycakes so soon?" It was just like the child to do something out of the ordinary, the opposite of what everyone else was doing. Single-minded though he was, he was a good boy and a more-than-able student, well on the path to becoming a powerful Dyrrwed priest. Already, Manfred had been able to teach him a hundred verses and tales of their people, the Dumnonii. Of course, there were literally thousands more, but so far, the boy had memorized each and every one he'd been taught. No small feat for a child his age.

Dylan shrugged. "I was at the festival, warming my hands near the fire, when I heard someone calling my name." He pulled his hands up inside of the thick brown woolen cloak he wore as if, with the telling of the tale, the small fingers remembered how cold they had been. "I walked into the woods, down the path where the two tall stones stand watching the stream. I heard my name again." His eyes met Manfred's. "Then I saw a lady there."

Manfred grinned. "And what sort of lady did you find?"

"A wet one, Sir. She was just lying there under the water, smiling up at me. Then she started to talk, and her voice sounded like music. She told me I should be here, with you." He pulled his hands out of his cloak and tossed a green pebble up into the air with one hand and caught it with the other. When he showed his palms, the stone had vanished. He pushed his black hair out of his eyes and looked at Manfred again.

Manfred's grin faded. He took the boy by the shoulders and looked at him carefully, judging the truth of what was said. Dylan's gaze never wavered. Manfred ran a hand through his silver streaked bright red beard. Had he heard correctly? Had the raven goddess of the water, Morrigu herself, spoken to the boy? Manfred sucked in his breath. *It truly is a special night.*

At that moment, to his left, one of his churls came lumbering out of the barn, wiping his hands on a bit of ragged cloth. To his right, the midwife appeared at the door to the keep, a soft bundle in her arms.

"The new foal has arrived, my Lord. She's as white as a fair summer cloud, she is." The churl grinned broadly, displaying two rows of uneven teeth, then turned and walked back to the barn.

"An' I 'ave more news fer ye, Sir. Yer child has finally come." The midwife placed the babe in his arms and pulled the blanket away from the small face. As she did so, a hawk flew overhead, crying to the night. The midwife jumped, then made a quick sign for protection.

Manfred stared up at the bird and a shiver ran along his spine. All the signs were present: The appearance of a goddess. The birth of a white foal at the same moment as the babe. The hawk...

It could only mean one thing. The child would be triply blessed by the gods and goddesses, with the powers of healing at its command.

"How is Lady Rhea? Did she fare well?" he asked, his voice a ragged whisper.

"Oh, Sir, she done jest fine." The midwife smiled kindly. "She's a-sleepin' already."

He looked at the sky again as the hawk continued to circle overhead, now joined by what appeared to be a large raven. "Morrigu," he whispered.

Sparks from the fire lifted with the wind and mixed with the stars. Still the birds flew steady. When Manfred realized the midwife was still speaking to him, he shook his head to clear it. "What was it you said?"

"I says I'm very sorry it's a girl-child. I know how disappointed ye must be." She pulled her homespun shawl tighter around her shoulders as light snowflakes began to fall.

Manfred waved her away impatiently. "Nonsense, woman. Girls have their value, and my daughter will aspire to greatness." He puffed his chest out. "She will be a leader of the Dumnonii. Nay, of all the Keltoi tribes." He gestured to the sky. "Tell me you don't see the signs!" Manfred lowered his hand. He ran a rough finger down the babe's cheek and stroked the downy thatch of dark red hair covering her head. "Leave the babe with me and go watch over my wife in case she wakes."

"But, Sir. It's gettin' much too cold fer the child to be out here." She glanced around, as if hoping for someone to support her position. "Sir?"

Manfred's expression grew dark. "You heard me. Off with you." When she hesitated, he barked, "Now!" The midwife took a step back, then turned and ran into the hall, her shawl trailing behind her.

He chuckled, then gazed down at his new daughter. "Dylan," he whispered as he crouched down. "This is an important lesson and I want you to remember it. Look at this babe. Life is sacred. It should never be taken from another in vain or for the purpose of calling up healthy crops." He sighed. "There are those who disagree with me on this matter, but, as your teacher, it's important to me that you understand."

"I'll remember, Sir." Dylan leaned forward, his eyes wide as he looked at the baby. "She's beautiful. Prettier even than the lady in the stream."

Manfred laughed. "Of course, she is. And, because of your vision, I have decided to name her Maere, after the water spirit."

Dylan smiled proudly. But as he continued to watch the babe, his smile faded. He touched the child's tiny hand and whispered, "I swear by all the gods and goddesses that I will protect her for you and the Lady Rhea." He raised his eyes to Manfred. "Always."

I hope you enjoyed this sneak peek of
Pagan Fire
Oracle Dreams Trilogy: Book 3

Visit Amazon.com to purchase your copy!

ABOUT THE AUTHOR

In addition to her Oracle Dreams Trilogy, Teri Barnett is the bestselling author of the Bijoux Mystery Series and the upcoming Lac Voo Mystery Series. Both cozy mystery series are set in sleepy tourist towns on the Lake Michigan shoreline. She's also the creator of Cats & More: Adult Coloring Book Series, a Reiki Master Teacher, and has written numerous non-fiction books about the practice and teaching of Reiki. Other non-fiction works include *How to be a Kickass Goddess: Twelve Steps to Owning Your Life* and the accompanying *Kickass Goddess Journal*, because you always need to journal when you're a Kickass Goddess.

All of Teri's books can be found on Amazon.

And if being an author isn't enough, Teri is also an award winning artist and nationally recognized commercial interior designer who brings a lifetime of learning and exploration to her writing and workshops. Born and raised in Michigan, Teri currently resides in Indiana where she writes books, does cool art, crochets too many shawls and blankets, and hangs out with Black Cat Lou, her bossy black cat. BCL is the inspiration for Griselda, Morgan Hart's rescue cat in the Bijoux Mystery Series, who makes her debut in Book 2, *Mystics are Murder*.

When Teri isn't busy working on her next book or redesigning the world, you can find her doing the artist thing in her studio, tromping through the forest, hanging with her kids and grandkids, or riding through the corn tunnels of Indiana on her motorcycle.

You can visit Teri online at www.teribarnett.com to learn more about her books, subscribe to her newsletter, and/or just to drop her a line to say hello.

TERI BARNETT
COMPLETE BOOK LIST

ORACLE DREAMS TRILOGY
Historical/Paranormal Time Travel Romance Trilogy

Through the Mists of Time: Oracle Dreams Trilogy Book 1

In 1865 London, Valerie Sherwood Brooks embarks on a tour of Italy where she is catapulted back in time to the ancient city of Pompeii and into the arms of a mysterious man who will alter her very destiny.

With a romantic heart and yearning for adventure, Valerie is overjoyed at the prospect of leaving London for the excitement of Italy, even if it means traveling with her overly protective parents and rambunctious little brother. Despite a childhood accident that has left her in need of a cane, Valerie is determined to explore the ancient ruins of Pompeii on her own. But when an earthquake shatters their visit to the Old City, Valerie is hurled back in time to 79 A.D.

Thrust into a world of intrigue and danger, Valerie is forced into servitude in the grand home of the darkly handsome Christos Marcellus. As Valerie tries to keep her wits about her, she is torn between her complex feelings for Christos and her need to get back to her own time.

Knowing the coming eruption of Vesuvius will mean doom and destruction, Valerie is faced with a life and death decision. Will she make the right choice in time?

Shadow Dreams: Oracle Dreams Trilogy Book 2

In the village of Paran, in the peaceful realm of Keilah, Bethany M'Doro embarks on a voyage to the Earth plane, to the year 1875, in search of a man who has the power to save her or destroy her.

Widowed with a young daughter, Bethany M'Doro possesses a unique ability to see into the past and her clairvoyant gifts make her invaluable on archeological digs. Her team's most recent discovery—an ornate comb buried under a pile of charred bones—sparks a vision of the ancient evil cult of Eitel, known for stealing children's souls. Although it was believed the cult was destroyed centuries ago, Bethany senses it has been resurrected by a diabolical new leader.

Bethany returns home from the expedition, to discover her worst fear has been realized. Her daughter Sarah has gone missing along with several other children from the village. It can only be the evil cult Eitel. Desperate to find them, Bethany's visions guide her to the Earth plane, to Devil's Gate, Nevada in 1875. There she encounters Connor Jessup, the only man who has the power to help her. But Connor is tormented by his own personal demons and a tragic past that continues to haunt him.

Bethany now faces the greatest challenge of her life. Can she heal Connor and convince him to travel back with her to Paran to find Eitel's lair and save Sarah and the other children from certain death? Or will her daughter be lost forever?

Pagan Fire: Oracle Dreams Trilogy Book 3

In 883 A.D., in a secluded convent in Great Britain, Maere cu Llwyr embarks on a journey back to her home of Tintagel, Cornwall with a powerful warrior who claims to be her long lost betrothed.

Dylan mac Connall survived the slaughter of his family by a traitor to their clan. A young boy at the time, he was rescued by a wise woman who taught him the ways of magic and warned him of the perils that lay ahead if he chose a path of revenge. But Dylan can no longer heed the advice of his foster mother and is determined to avenge his family and find the spirited girl he loved in his youth.

Raised in an abbey by the Sisters of Saint Columba, Maere cu Llwyr is ready to take her full vows and become a nun. But when the warrior Dylan arrives and claims to be her rightful betrothed, Maere is shocked and wary of what her future will bring. A wee child when she was abducted from her village, Maere has blocked the memories of that horrific night. She has no recollection of the powerful ancient magic dormant inside her, or of the handsome man determined to unlock both Maere's mind and her power.

As Maere and Dylan travel back to Tintagel, they must face the mercurial goddess Morrigu, dangerous Viking raiders, and the traitor who destroyed their families. Can Maere and Dylan survive the battles to come and find their way back home and to each other? Or will they be forever separated by forces outside of their control?

BIJOUX MYSTERY SERIES

Romance is Murder: Bijoux Mystery Series Book 1

A dead diva, a rotten romance, and a town full of nosy neighbors…

Morgan Hart is home. A former homicide detective in Detroit, Morgan is back in her old hometown of Bijoux, Michigan to take over the reins of Sheriff from her dad, Able. The town has undergone quite a transformation since she lived here with new, kitschy shops along Main Street and a burgeoning tourist trade. Even the iconic pink Firefly Bed & Breakfast has jumped on the bandwagon and is hosting a romance writers' convention with some of the biggest names in the 'happily ever after' biz.

Morgan hopes to ease into her new job, new cottage, and new life – after all, Bijoux hasn't had a murder in a hundred years. But all of Morgan's plans go up in smoke when the biggest diva of the romance world is found dead.

As Morgan and her deputy, JJ Jones, begin their investigation, the townspeople have no qualms about telling her how to do her job, including Caleb Joseph, owner of the local bookstore who is far too nosy (and attractive) for Morgan's comfort.

With a murder to solve and the town in turmoil, Morgan will have to rely on her big city cop skills to catch a killer harboring a hate for happy endings.

Mystics are Murder: Bijoux Mystery Series Book 2

What do you do when your star murder witness only speaks 'Meow?'

Who could predict it would happen again? Morgan Hart didn't expect her first day as police captain of Bijoux, Michigan, the sleepy lakeside town where she grew up, would include a murder, even though that's just what happened. But with the killer behind bars, Morgan can take a breath and start painting her cozy cottage.

Or so she hopes.

When a fortune-telling mystic is found dead at Bijoux's Walk into the Light Psychic Gathering, Morgan and her deputy, JJ Jones, are called in to investigate. The trouble is Morgan's only witness is Griselda, a black cat with blood on her paws.

While every psychic in town claims to know what the cat 'knows,' Morgan relies on her own instincts to sniff out the suspects while dodging her conflicting feelings for local bookshop owner and town hunk, Caleb Joseph. And with her dad, Able's, upcoming wedding to Zoe Buffet, Bijoux's most famous clairvoyant and coffee cake queen, Morgan is under the gun to figure out which mystic is the murderer before the couple says I do.

Cupcakes are Murder: Bijoux Mystery Series Book 3

A cupcake conundrum, a culinary queen on the edge, and a cold-case killer on the loose…

Morgan Hart is settling into her job as police captain of Bijoux, the quaint and quirky tourist town nestled on the Lake Michigan shoreline. Murders have been solved, kittens have been rescued, and progress has been made in the renovation of her cozy cottage by the beach. Despite her grief and ongoing frustration over her husband's unsolved murder six years ago, Morgan hopes an overdue break in the case will finally lead to justice, even if it means exposing a betrayal that could leave her reeling.

Meanwhile, Morgan needs to keep a sharp eye on the upcoming Baker's Dozen Hometown Cupcake Bake-off and TV special hosted by British baking superstar Sassy McComas, aka The Queen of Cupcakes. Rumor has it, Queen Sass is secretly searching for a fresh face to host a new TV show and the competitors vying for the top spot include Bijoux's own pastry princess, Hannah Bellamy.

But when one of the top challengers in the Cupcake Bake-off turns up dead, Morgan has to sift through the evidence and stop the killer before they strike again and threaten to topple Queen Sass from her throne.

Pumpkins are Murder: Bijoux Mystery Series Book 4

A dead carver, dueling witches, and more tricks than treats…

Bijoux, Michigan is serious about Halloween.

Known as the most haunted town on the Lake Michigan shoreline, Bijoux hosts the annual Pumpkins and Poe Festival—the town's annual homage to Edgar Allan Poe and all things spooky. Pumpkin carvers from around the country flock to Bijoux, slicing and dicing their way into Halloween history. But when one of the carvers turns up dead with a jack-o-lantern on their head and a note with the word Nevermore scrawled in orange ink pinned to their apron, police captain Morgan Hart is called in to investigate.

After solving multiple murders at three previous Bijoux events, the beleaguered police captain steps into the fray once again, along with her down-in-the-dumps deputy, JJ Jones, recently ditched by his girlfriend, local cupcake maven, Hannah Bellamy. Meanwhile, Morgan's own "weak and weary" heart keeps getting tested by Caleb Joseph, owner of the Raven's Nest bookstore. The too-hot-for-his-own-good former Gothic Lit professor has made a hobby out of snooping around Morgan's cases.

It's up to Morgan to thwart various Halloween hijinks around Bijoux while preventing the town from panicking as she tries to catch a killer who's turned "trick or treat" into the darkest diversion of all—murder.

Mistletoe is Murder: Bijoux Mystery Series Book 5

Skeletons with secrets, prohibition pirates, and holiday hijinks…

Morgan Hart is hoping for a boring Christmas. After eight months of murderous mayhem in her hometown of Bijoux, Michigan, she just wants to snuggle under a warm blanket in front of a cozy fire, with a good book, a hot chocolate (extra marshmallows of course), and Griselda purring beside her. She might even work up the nerve to ask Caleb Joseph over for dinner. Cal, the attractive owner of the Raven's Nest bookstore, has become a good friend since Morgan moved back home to take on the job of police captain.

A bestselling mystery author, Cal recently purchased the old Lawrence Mansion on the edge of town and plans to throw a big Christmas Eve bash. But Morgan's holiday plans—romantic and otherwise—go up in smoke when dark and shadowy secrets are revealed during the clean-up of the 19th century-built home. Can Morgan and Cal uncover the ghostly truth or are they destined for a disastrous deck-the-halls?

CATS & MORE: ADULT COLORING BOOKS

Volume 1: Angsty Cats

Volume 2: Snarky Cats

Volume 3: Mandala Cats

Volume 4: Spooky Cats

Volume 5: Jingle Cats

Volume 6: Mystery Cats

Volume 7: More Mystery Cats

Volume 8: Coloring is Murder *(based on the Bestselling Bijoux Mystery Series)*

Volume 9: Cat Facts

Volume 10: Camping Tarot

Volume 11: Cosmic Cats

Volume 12: Crochet & Cats

NON-FICTION

Visit ReikiOne.com, PresenceandShadow.com, and/or SacredPriestess Journeys.com for more information.

How to Be a Kickass Goddess: Twelve Steps to Owning Your Life

What would your life look like if you owned it? REALLY owned it? Who would you be? How would you live? What would you do? In a straightforward, down-to-earth style, How to Be a Kickass Goddess: Twelve Steps to Owning Your Life takes you on a journey directly into You - everything you are and everything you can be. Now, grab this book and get busy. The world needs all the Kickass Goddesses she can get!

How to be a Kickass Goddess: Companion Journal

Beginnings: ReikiOne First Degree Manual

This manual covers the basics of Reiki training and practice, including history, principles, hand positions, and treatment guidelines. Also included is a brief introduction to the chakras and using crystals with Reiki.

The Deeper Journey: ReikiOne Second Degree Manual

The ReikiOne Second Degree Manual includes the three symbols traditionally associated with this degree, explanations and their use, methods of distance healing, sending Reiki through time and space, combining symbols for greater effect, the chakra system, the human aura, and a suggested reading list.

Reiki Master: ReikiOne Third Degree Manual Part A by Teri Barnett, Reiki Master Teacher

This book contains the 4th symbol, its use for Reiki treatments, a discussion of what it means to be a Reiki Master, and how to use crystal grids with Reiki.

Reiki Master Teacher: ReikiOne Third Degree Manual Part B

The Master Teacher Manual contains all the information your students need for stepping into Reiki Master Teacher - A review of the 4th symbol (plus additional data on this symbol), the 5th symbol for attunements, attunement instructions (individual and group), methods and ethics of teaching, getting in touch with your inner teacher, marketing ideas, an extensive reading list, and much more.

The Reiki Teacher's Handbook

A composite of all the ReikiOne Manuals, the Reiki Teacher's Handbook takes your teaching a step further. This book provides you with all the tools you'll need to teach Reiki. Written from the experienced perspective of a master Teacher of the Usui Shiki Ryoho method, you'll find this book adapts easily to other forms of Reiki and can grow with you as you progress on your teaching path.

www.ingramcontent.com/pod-product-compliance
Lightning Source LLC
Chambersburg PA
CBHW020116180626
46812CB00006B/2621